Monterey Bay Mystery

AMANDA WARREN COZY ANIMAL MYSTERY
BOOK ONE

SEREN STAR GOODE

Dedicated to my mum for her complete faith in everything I do and for sharing her love of cozy British mysteries.

ONE

Stars Above

G rok arched his back, feeling the stretch from the tips of his paws to the tingling sensation in his shoulder blades. With a swish of his tail, the long fringe waved, stirring the damp night air. He sniffed. He was still alone.

Turning once, twice, three times, the large cat settled back into the stake-out spot on the roof, the wood shingles still radiating the heat from the day's sun. He resisted the urge to roll onto his back. He was a professional with work to do. Straightening, he resumed vigil on his home across the street.

It had been late afternoon when a key had turned in the lock on the back door. Thinking it was Alexandra finally returning home, he had overcome his displeasure at her leaving him behind and had rushed to the door in an unforgivable show of enthusiasm.

As the door swung open, he heard the vile male

human's voice talking on a phone, and he realized his mistake.

The interloping neighbor had been sneaking into the house whenever Alexandra was gone, bringing female humans and doing unspeakable things.

As he had done a thousand times before, Grok quietly stalked through the shadows, unsheathed his claws, and moved closer to his prey. Suddenly, his head had grown cloudy, he'd stumbled, his balance off. The episodes weren't as frequent, but they left him bewildered and vulnerable, and he quickly retreated, slipping out the cat door.

At one time in his life, Grok would have defended his home and family, fighting off intruders. At least, he thought he remembered doing that. It was yet another of the fuzzy memories trapped inside his head.

Despite his extensive memory loss, Grok knew he wasn't an average cat. He was more intelligent than all the animals around him, including the humans, naturally. He could understand everything humans said to each other, no matter the language, but Alexandra was the only one who could understand him. She had explained that cats talking to humans was not normal on this planet.

So, then—where was Grok from?

Never one to bypass a mystery, Alexandra had gone searching for answers and never returned.

Grok hissed. Angry that once again, he was powerless. He was forced out into the foggy night while the vile male completed his disgusting human mating rituals.

Time passed. The vigil grew tiring, and Grok stopped

resisting the urge and rolled onto his back. Basking in the warmth of the wood shingles, the cat stared up between the clouds at the starry sky. Somehow, they seemed more familiar than the neighborhood around him. And not for the first time, he wondered who he was.

TWO

New In Town

As Amanda Warren turned onto Route One and headed south towards Monterey, the Pacific Ocean spread out before her like a cool gray blanket. She pulled the big pink van off the highway, rolling to a stop and flicking on the hazard lights.

Emotions swelled like waves at her first look at the water.

She fished around the van's cab for the box of tissues. She hadn't cried this much when she caught her husband cheating, but the prospect of seeing her sister for the first time in twenty years left her a blubbering mess.

Why didn't she stay in touch? Swiping at her eyes, Amanda asked herself the more important question: *was she ready to see her now?*

Growing up orphaned and landlocked in Ohio, the ocean called to her and her twin, Alexandra. Enticing and mysterious. It became the center of their plan: escape their smothering aunt, make it to California, and become famous. In their teen view of the world, life started when you made it here. Of course, all their information came from watching Veronica Mars and 90210 reruns. They didn't know anyone from the West Coast. But that hadn't stopped them from making plans.

Then, one bad decision on Amanda's part destroyed that fragile dream.

Her memory flashed back to that day. Amanda was on her way to break up with her boyfriend when Alexandra texted that she had officially turned down her scholarship and was at the station waiting for her so they could "blow this town." Amanda hadn't turned up at the station. Instead, she had cowered at her new fiancé's apartment until after the bus departed. Amanda and Alexandra had that mythical twin connection, almost psychic, and Amanda had been sure by not turning up, Alexandra would stay. But she hadn't.

Amanda blew her nose into the tissue as the orange ball dipped to the ocean's edge, casting amber rays across the vast expanse of the Monterey Bay. A glance at the grooming van's instrument panel showed the fuel gauge empty. She'd been living on instant noodles and gas fumes and had put her last few dollars into the tank before getting off the 101. She was so close now. She would make these last miles, even if she had to get out and push.

If her sister rejected her apology, she'd be pushing the van away from Alexandra's house.

She tapped down the critical voice and put the gear in drive, heading south again.

It was dark when Amanda arrived in Ocean Wood, on the very tip of the Monterey Peninsula.

A cold, thick fog rolled in, keeping pace with the van as she drove slowly down the narrow residential streets. It was too dark to see the postcard addressed to her aunt that she had taped to the dashboard, but she didn't need it; she had memorized Alexandra's address long ago.

Her phone rang, and Amanda slammed on the van's brakes. She searched the cab, flinging old coffee cups, sandwich wrappers, and her map as she followed the sound. The number was primarily used for business, but two weeks ago, she sent her phone number in a reply to her sister's postcard, and ever since then she'd been jumping to respond whenever it rang.

Stretching her fingers, she brushed the phone on the floor. Pushing, she swept it up and squinted at the numbers.

"Ugh." That number was known.

She tossed the phone back on the floor and released the brake. Glancing back out at the street and the tightly packed wood houses with ornate trim, she continued looking for the address.

"Finally, thirty-forty." She muttered under her breath, her fingers beating an erratic rhythm on the steering wheel. The house was smaller than she expected and older. She always thought Alexandra would have a home by the ocean. It was almost a mile from the shore. Not for the first time, Amanda wondered what her sister had done with her life. Who had she become?

There was no place to park. Most homes didn't have

garages, leaving the street jammed with parked cars and work trucks. But her sister's place had a gravel drive that led past the side of the house, so she edged up onto the curb and turned into the tight entrance.

Suddenly, her headlights illuminated an old shed at the back of the house. She had pulled in too far. Before Amanda could back out, the Pink Pup's engine gave a wheeze and stalled.

Well, she had made it. She refused to think about what she would do if her sister didn't live here anymore. She had exhausted all her resources to get to this point.

Taking a deep breath, Amanda glanced into the rearview mirror. She smoothed her auburn brows and tugged a little too hard on a wild strand of frizzy hair that had escaped her sloppy bun.

Anxiety and excitement warred inside her.

Now she was here, all the rehearsed speeches in her head disappeared. What good were they anyway? How do you admit you were wrong to the one person you couldn't lie to?

"Okay, let's just do this." She said to the empty cab of the van, then yanked open the door and jumped out. She didn't know if it was nerves or the chilled air, but her whole body shuddered, and she felt exposed.

She picked her way back down the drive to the front of her sister's house and studied the porch. There were no lights on inside.

Gathering her nerve, she slowly made her way up the steps. The faint glow of the streetlamp across the street couldn't penetrate the darkness of the covered porch. She could just make out a curved loveseat and a small table framed in plants. The organic shapes left haunting shadows on the wood paneling.

As Amanda reached the front step, the whole porch was flooded with light. Relief swept through her. Someone was home.

Reaching up to knock, she noticed the door ajar. She knocked anyway, the force pushing the door open.

"Hello?" Amanda waited politely at the entrance for a response. None came.

Knocking again. "Hello? Alexandra?" Amanda called out louder and waited. She could see a light switch and a small table near the door through the large crack between the door and the jam. She leaned in and listened.

It was quiet in the house.

She knocked harder this time, ensuring she accidentally pushed the door open.

"Yoo-hoo! Anyone home?" She called out, bold now that it was becoming evident that no one was. Disappointment washed over her until she spotted a row of photographs on a table by the door. Excited, she flipped on the entryway's light switch and leaned far over the threshold.

On the table was a photo of two identical young women in caps and gowns with huge grins posing for the camera. Their arms wrapped around each other. Amanda remembered the feel of her skin glowing from the sun and the sweat trickling down her back under the robe. But they hadn't cared. They had graduated high school, and they were finally free. That is one of the last good memories she had with her sister.

This was Alexandra's house, and she had kept this photo—looked at it daily.

Relief swept through Amanda's body, and she sagged against the door frame. She hadn't been forgotten.

A sound came from inside the house.

"Hello?" Emboldened by the photo, Amanda stepped over the threshold, moving closer to the table. Beside the pictures, a knit hat partially hid a black spiral notebook with an elastic strap around it. Stuck to the book's cover was a post-it note that read, "Start here."

Amanda picked up the book, curious about the Alice in Wonderland warning. The hat was stuck to the metal spiral and came with it, dangling from a bit of pulled yarn. A sound came from deeper in the house as Amanda worked to untangle the hat.

"Alexandra? Is that you?" She didn't want to scare her sister, but just announcing herself felt weird. She did it anyway. "It's Amanda."

Amanda moved further into the living room, forgetting the book. "I'm sorry for coming in. The door was unlocked." She felt weird talking to herself.

Amanda backed into a room on the left side of the entryway, keeping her eyes on the hallway on the opposite side.

She stepped up on a rug and passed a desk and the arm of a worn yellow office chair. The light from the entryway didn't reach into this room, and Amanda wished she had taken the time to look for another light switch.

She tripped and stumbled backward. Looking down at the floor, she stared at the hand she had tripped over.

Why was a hand on the floor?

It took a minute to register that the hand was attached to an arm and a body. Next to the couch, a man's body lay contorted on the rug, his eyes open and lifeless.

The scream started before Amanda reached the door, and she was across the street before it stopped.

THREE

The Neighbors

Amanda stood across the street, shaking as the neighbor's house lights came on and heads popped out front doors.

She needed to call the police.

After several attempts to enter the three numbers, it connected. Her voice shook as she rattled off the address and her name. Someone assured her a car would arrive soon.

Amanda hung up and exhaled. Her body felt like jelly.

"Hey, are you okay?"

Amanda turned towards the woman. The short octogenarian had a motorcycle helmet tucked under an arm. She was dressed head to toe in black leather with a red bandana and had spiky white hair flattened on one side.

"You don't look so good. Maybe you should sit down."

Amanda's butt hit the sidewalk, and she clutched the hat and notebook to her chest.

The lady crouched down beside her. "Better?"

"Yeah, there was a—" Amanda stared at the closed door across the street and shuddered, "A body."

"A what? Where?" She glanced around, dropping the helmet and putting a hand on Amanda's shoulder to steady herself.

"In my sister's house. Oh, Buckeyes, she could still be in there. I need to go check." Amanda pointed across the street and tried to work up the nerve to follow through and return to the house.

Why was the door closed? She didn't remember shutting it behind her. Maybe she did it and forgot? She didn't remember crossing the street either.

"Your sister—Alexandra, are you okay? That's your house." The woman squeezed her shoulder.

"Oh, no, I'm not Alexandra. She's my twin."

"You don't say!" The spiky-haired woman pulled back and studied Amanda's face. "Well, what do you know? I couldn't tell in the dark, but it's real obvious up close. I'm not sure why I didn't see it. The hair alone should have tipped me off."

Amanda swiped at the frizzy red strand hanging in her face again and tucked it behind her ear. Despite craving every piece of knowledge she could glean, she shook off the instinct to ask about Alexandra's hair.

"What's happening? Is everything okay?" A pair of rainbow crocs speckled with white dust appeared next to her. Amanda looked up at the heavy-set man in basketball shorts and a tank top. His long dark hair was liberally salted with grey and hung around his shoulders.

Amanda pushed to her feet and swiped at the dirt on her bottom. She steeled her nerves. She needed to go back and find her sister.

"Uh, a little help here?" The spiky-haired older woman asked, holding up her arms.

Amanda and the man grabbed her hands and helped the lady to stand, ignoring the creaks and pops her joints emitted.

"Whew! At my age, you never know if you'll be able to get back up again." Under the pale light from the street-lamp, the joke seeped into the fog, pushing it back and warming a little pocket of air where they stood until the woman added, "She found a body."

"A body?" The man swung to Amanda, eyes wide. "Who was it? Someone we know? Where was it? Was it a heart attack? Bob always says I'm going to give myself one of those." The man leaned in, and his voice dropped to a conspiratorial whisper. "Was it murder?"

Amanda stepped away.

"Oh, stop it. The girl just called the police. How would she know if it's murder?" Dot slapped a hand on Rainbow Croc's side, then turned to Amanda. "It wasn't murder, was it?"

"Her name is Alexandra." Rainbow Crocs gave Amanda a baffled shrug and then turned an amused smile to the octogenarian. "Starting to lose those memory cells from all your racing?" He got another slap on his side from the woman.

"You hush. She isn't Alexandra. She is her twin sister,

Amanda." The woman imparted this information like it was a juicy bit of gossip.

While the man's face registered shock, skepticism, and then surprise acknowledgment of her identity, Amanda made her decision. "I'm going back there to look for Alexandra." It was voiced with more conviction than she felt. What if Rainbow Crocs was right, and it was a murder—would the killer still be there?

"If you aren't her, then I've not seen Alexandra around for a couple days. Her car isn't here, and if she were home, she would have on her regular lights, not the security lights. I doubt she's in there." Rainbow Crocs seemed convinced, and Amanda wanted to hug him in relief.

"Guess I need to introduce myself. I'm Dot. I live one street over." The woman pointed behind the house on the left of Alexandra's. "And this is Frank Guzman." She pointed to the Rainbow Crocs man.

"Saw you arrive in that pink monster of a van. I thought it was for one of Alexandra's cases. What the heck is that thing?" Frank asked.

Amanda was bewildered by their casual banter in the face of this catastrophe. But she was used to questions about her van, and it was distracting her from thinking about the body she had found. "It's called the Pink Pup. I'm a groomer, 'Pink Power Wash & Groom.' Mostly, I groom dogs, but sometimes other animals." Curious, she added, "What type of case would my sister have?"

"That makes sense, but what are those things hanging off the sides?" Frank unconsciously scratched his ear.

Frank either didn't hear or didn't care to elaborate on Alexandra's work.

"What van?" Dot interrupted.

"It's parked on the side of the house. You can't see it from here, but it's something to see. The whole thing looks like a giant dog!" Frank turned back to Amanda, waiting for her answer.

Amanda was defensive of the Pink Pup. "There's a graphics wrap on the van, so it looks like a big pink puppy, but my ex-husband thought it wasn't enough and had the faux fur ears installed." Amanda didn't like thinking about the ex or anything connected to him. But he was the reason she had gotten into the grooming business. He was also the reason she had left Ohio.

"What is going on?" A third neighbor arrived. He was the only one dressed appropriately for the weather with a rain jacket over a fleece, hiking pants, and work boots.

"She says she found a body." Dot quickly disclosed.

The Fleece Jacket man gasped. "Who was it?"

Amanda shook her head. Everyone seemed more interested in gossip than they were shocked about a body being discovered.

Dot pointed to the man in fleece. "Amanda, this is Anh Nguyen. Did you say you called the police?"

She gave a quick nod and drew in a shuddering breath. "They are on their way."

"Sure, they are." As he rolled his eyes, Frank shifted from side to side in his rainbow Crocs. "Like they care. No one even turned up when I reported my break-in and theft."

"It wasn't a break-in. You slipped in those funny rubber shoes you wear and knocked over your planters. Police have better things to do than pander to you." Dot narrowed her eyes as she looked up at the man who was at least two feet taller than her.

"It was a break-in. And they stole my boots." Frank drew out the words and gave the group a mulish look, then huffed at the lack of sympathy.

"There was an accident on The One, south of Carmel, this evening. They may still be working it." Anh stuffed his hands into the pockets of his fleece jacket.

"No, that's the Sheriff's office. The Ocean Wood police are who should respond to this." Frank pointed out. Then he turned on Amanda, "Was it a man or woman? Could you describe them?"

Amanda paled while the image of the man lying on the floor was etched into her memory forever. She didn't think she could repeat what she saw without getting sick. She shook her head. "Man."

"A man. Who on the street is missing?" Frank turned to Anh and Dot.

"Why do you think it's someone from here?" Dot wrinkled her nose. "Could be a stranger. It could be one of Alexandra's cases. Maybe it was a mafia hit."

One of Alexandra's cases? Amanda thought.

Before she could ask a question, Frank eagerly tapped Dot's arm. "We should go check it out. We know everyone. We'd be able to identify if it was someone local.

"We should not disturb the crime scene." Amanda had watched enough mystery shows to know that much.

"So, it *was* a murder!" Frank pounced on the idea.

"Where is everyone else?" Anh blurted out. "Why aren't all the neighbors out looking at what is happening?"

"You know people. They just don't care anymore. Not like us. Besides, the Bay Area people aren't here because it's a weekday." Dot pointed to the dark building on the right of Alexandra's house.

Then she nodded to Anh, "You are here."

For Amanda's benefit, she pointed to a house behind them, across from the Bay Area people. "That is Anh and Amy's cottage."

"Franks here with Bob in their Craftsman." Dot pointed her finger behind her at the house whose fence we were leaning against. "I don't know why Colleen isn't out here. Her light is on, and she is one of our nosiest neighbors. Maybe her husband is home. He wouldn't care." Dot pointed across the street to the house to the left of her sister's, and as if by magic, the lights in the house went out.

"Huh, that was fun." Dot blew on the end of her finger like it was a gun.

"What are you doing here? You don't even live on this block." Anh asked.

"I was heading home from the racetrack and saw this crazy woman screaming and running down the street."

Amanda couldn't dispute the description but whispered, "Across the street."

"Yeah, across the street, that makes it so much better. So, I stopped to see if I could help."

The sound of a siren filled the air.

"Ah shoot. Now the police are here, and we can't sneak a peek at the body." Frank sounded a little too disappointed in Amanda's sense of self-preservation, and she moved away from him.

"Well, I've been in one of these shows before. I don't want to spend an hour hanging around waiting to give a statement—so I'm going to go home now; Albert is waiting." Dot gave them all a wave and jogged to her motorcycle. Amanda hadn't spotted the bike before. It was a scaled model rather than a full-sized bike. Quicker than Amanda thought possible, Dot hopped on and rode off.

"Well, that's not very community-minded of her. I should report her to the police as fleeing the scene." Amanda couldn't imagine that Frank was serious.

But Dot was gone, and a police car with sirens wailing pulled around the corner and stopped in the center of the street. Another car came from the other direction and parked facing the first, blocking the road. Cops got out of both sides of the car, hands on the guns at their hips, and approached the group.

FOUR

The Body, Again

Amanda's nerves were at a breaking point. She bit her lip and mentally scolded herself for being too cowardly to return to the house and ensure Alexandra wasn't inside, trapped, or hurt. Now she was waiting for the cops inside the house to tell her what had happened and if her sister was safe.

A third car pulled up, and a man in a suit exited and entered the house.

"That's our detective, Adam Kim," Frank said to Amanda.

"You just have one?"

"Two, they take turns being on call. We are lucky to have them being the size of our town."

"How do you know this?" Anh asked, hands still stuffed in his jacket pockets.

"Back in my suit-wearing days, I was on the city council for a long time."

They continued to wait.

"Oh, ho, that's interesting." Frank chuckled under his breath as a fourth car pulled up, and a woman in a formal police uniform got out. Everyone on the job stood a little taller, and those who weren't busy found something to do.

"Who is that?" Amanda couldn't resist asking.

"That is Ocean Wood's Chief of Police, Gina Rodriguez. Probably here to check on your sister."

"Why would she be checking on my sister?"

"Because they used to be partners on the force."

Amanda whipped around to face him. *Was her sister a cop?*

She processed this information while the detective exited the house and stopped before the chief. They spoke for a moment, and then the detective called Amanda over.

"I'm Detective Adam Kim. This is Chief of Police Gina Rodriguez. We want to ask you a few questions." At Amanda's nod, the detective continued. "You found the body?"

She nodded again.

Detective Kim just stared at her. He was dressed in a pressed suit and looked so well put together that you couldn't tell if this was the beginning or end of his shift. His straight black hair was slicked in place, and with a lack of lines on his face, Amanda could only tell from his efficiency that he had been doing this job for a while. After several seconds, the man added. "Can you tell me what you saw?"

Amanda blushed and realized what he had been waiting for. "Sorry. Of course." Voice shaking, she took a calming breath. "I knocked. No one answered. Oh, and the door wasn't closed or locked. It pushed open. It was dark inside."

"The light was on when the officers arrived."

"Yes, that was me. When the door pushed open, I could see...well, I turned on the light, and when I called out, and no one answered, I went in."

"Why?" The detective asked.

Amanda flinched. Why had she gone in? Optimism? Sentimentality? Stupidity? Pick one. "With the door open, I was worried about my sister. I called out and just went a few feet into the house when I tripped." She shuddered as an image of the limp hand flashed in her memory. "I tripped over the hand. I didn't even realize what it was until I saw the man's whole body curled up on the floor. I think I screamed. Ran. I called the police and waited across the street for you guys to arrive."

Suddenly cold, Amanda clutched the hat and book tighter, hugging her arms to her chest. The chief's stony gaze was unnerving.

"What did the supposed body look like?" the detective asked.

Amanda frowned at the question. "Well, you saw, white guy about fifty, dark hair. Tan pants and a collared shirt."

The detective noted everything in his notebook and then repeated his questions again, studying her face as she responded the second time.

When he asked for the third time for Amanda to describe what she found in the house, questioning if she was sure, Amanda blew out an exasperated sigh. "Why don't you believe me?"

Chief Rodriguez spoke for the first time. "Because there is no body in Alexandra's house and there is no sign of a break-in."

Amanda's jaw dropped. "No— But the man was there, on the rug in the front room, all dead and covered in ick."

Chief Rodriguez shared a look with the detective, then shook her head. The detective made a note in his book.

"We could take you in for making a false report." The chief's dark eyes narrowed, and her tone told Amanda she was seriously considering this action.

Amanda gulped. Without thought, she leaned away but managed to stop herself from taking a step back. "No, it was there. I'll show you." She moved towards the house.

The detective didn't budge as he continued. "Or we could arrest you for breaking and entering—"

"The door was open," Amanda whispered the interruption. She felt woozy and confused. Had she gotten so tired from driving she had hallucinated a body?

"—But I don't think your sister would appreciate that." The chief's tough facade relaxed briefly. "You are the exact image of Alexandra, except for the hair. If I didn't know her so well, I'd be convinced this was one of her jokes."

Amanda latched onto that information. Her sister's practical jokes were epic. But even this would be too far for her. "Do you know where she is? Can you give me her phone number?"

The chief cocked a brow and then shook her head.

Amanda couldn't tell if that was a "no" or an "I won't tell you." This woman had been the only person she had met in Ocean Wood so far who had known immediately that she was not Alexandra. Frank said they were police partners. Did she know about what had happened back in Ohio all those years ago? Did she know if her sister still hated her? Before she could work up the nerve to ask, the chief turned in her shiny black shoes and left.

The police started wrapping up their work and returning to their vehicles and Amanda wondered what happened next.

"I didn't even know that Alex had a sister." The detective closed his notebook.

"She does. Do you know where she is? When will she be back?" Amanda leaned in.

The detective shook his head. "If you want to know anything about her, I suggest you ask the chief. You have to see how suspicious the timing of your arrival is. No one knows you. Your sister is—" The detective hesitated as if choosing his word carefully, "—gone. And you turn up, claiming to find a body. If you didn't look just like Alexandra, I'm not sure I'd believe you were her sister."

Amanda held her breath as she waited for the detective's next words. Was she going to be arrested? She could prove they were sisters, but really, what difference would that make?

"You are fortunate that the chief doesn't want this pursued. You are free to go. But we are watching you. And we can't let you have access to the house. Do you have a place to stay?"

Amanda shook her head to clear the confusion. "No. I mean, yes. I can stay in my van." She pointed around the corner of the house.

The detective squinted to see the vehicle through the fog and darkness, then turned back to her. "I'm going to pretend I didn't hear that."

Detective Kim left her standing on the stoop. As the last car pulled away, Amanda looked back at the house. There was no evidence that anything had happened except that the front door was now closed and presumably locked.

What a weird night. With heavy feet, Amanda headed down the gravel drive to the Pink Pup. She was starving, her head hurt, her back was sore from driving for days, and she just wanted to blow up her air mattress and curl up in her sleeping bag.

The side door of the van was unlocked when she got there. Amanda was relieved not to have to search for the keys. Shoving her phone in her pocket, she pulled down the manual steps and slid open the door. She flipped on the light and screamed.

Sitting in a chair in the middle of her grooming van was the body.

FIVE

No Body Knows

In what was becoming the longest night ever, Amanda tucked the notebook under her arm as she stood in the same spot across the street and called the police again. She couldn't see the van from here, but that was okay because everyone who lived on the road could see her, and she wasn't going to stand in the dark with a body. Again.

At least it was the same body. A different body would have been worse.

"Better the body, you know," Amanda muttered with a nervous laugh that reminded her of how tired she was. She shivered in her thin jacket. At least now the police would know where the body from the house had gone. But how had it ended up in her van?

As the call connected, Amanda rattled off her information again. A horrible thought occurred to her: had her sister been in the house and moved the body?

She almost hung up the phone but didn't see how that would help her sister if she were involved.

The 911 operator had her repeat herself three times. Eventually, convinced it wasn't a hoax, the woman said a car was coming.

The man in the house had been dead. Amanda was sure of it. Freaked out as she was, she didn't remember much, but his eyes were open in a very dead way. No mistaking it. There was no way he could have gotten up and wandered out to her van. So how did he get there?

She was sure she had locked the Pink Pup. But maybe she hadn't. She was distracted when she arrived.

It was several minutes before police cars returned. Sirens off this time.

None of the neighbors came out.

Frank called out from inside his house and asked if she was okay. Amanda just waved him off.

Detective Kim got out of the car and walked to her. "What seems to be the problem now?"

Amanda knew the operator must have told him but accepted this was part of the process. "The body. It's in my van now."

"Another body?" The detective was skilled at being respectful and skeptical with the same look.

"No. The same body. A man." Why was this so hard for him to understand?

"Did you move him?"

"No, I'm not touching him." Amanda's voice came out shrill, and she found herself leaning away at the idea.

The detective shook his head. "Not what I meant. Did you move him from the house to your van?" As the detective spoke, the officers from the other car moved to either side of Amanda.

"Of course not. He was dead in the house and now, somehow, he is dead in my van." Okay, Amanda admitted to herself, that sounded strange when she said it out loud.

"We will check it out. Do you have your keys?"

Amanda shook her head. "You won't need them. I must have left it unlocked."

The detective nodded, and Amanda watched as he and another officer stalked carefully down the drive, the automatic light on the front porch coming on as they passed. The men disappeared into the fog and darkness at the side of the house.

The remaining two officers stayed with Amanda. Somehow, this felt more for the neighbor's protection than hers.

Several minutes later, Detective Kim emerged from the mist and shadows and came halfway back toward them before beckoning her to follow him. When she got close enough, he said, "Please, come with me."

Amanda clenched the book and hat to her chest with her elbows and folded her hands in front of her face, trying not to bite her knuckles as he led her back through the fog to the van. He indicated the open door. "Can you describe what you see?"

Amanda braced herself and stepped up to the portal.

Her grooming van was neatly organized. There was a large wash basin mounted to the back and a hydraulic grooming table secured in place. Even her personal items were strapped into the open space on the side, so they didn't fly around while she drove.

What was noticeably missing was a body.

Amanda leaned in to see if somehow it had fallen into a corner, which was ridiculous.

She drew back and felt her face flame. "I swear, it was there. The same one from the house. A tallish white man with dark hair, a dark blue shirt, and khaki trousers. Dead. Same as before, just a different place."

"When did you see him last?"

"Immediately before I called you. You had just left. I went to the van to sleep, and he was just there. Oh, and the chair. He was on the chair from the house. Are there fibers? Did you check for fibers?" Her voice rose higher with each sentence.

Detective Kim raised his hands in a soothing motion. "There is no evidence of a crime."

Amanda shook her head, a strand of frizzy red hair falling into her face, and she yanked it behind her ear, her voice raising in pitch. "I'm not making it up. I swear. Check for fibers, get swabs, or something. There was a body in here."

"What's going on?" The authoritative voice came from behind her.

Amanda's head sunk between her shoulders. She didn't turn around as Chief Rodriguez stepped up to the opening of the van. She still looked as pressed and fresh as if it was first thing in the morning, not almost midnight.

Detective Kim filled her in, and Amanda winced as she started questioning her own version of things.

The chief studied her.

"I don't know what game you are playing, but I think it is best if you move on. You can stay here tonight, but you need to find a new place in the morning."

Amanda was embarrassed but held her head high. She had seen a body. Twice. Calling the police was the right thing to do, even if it didn't feel that way.

"I understand, but I still want to find my sister. If there is anything you know about her whereabouts, I would appreciate knowing." The chief didn't say anything, but Amanda felt the waves of judgment rolling off her. The chief didn't like her.

"I want you to keep out of police investigations." Chief Rodriguez turned and left after the warning, again without a goodbye.

Wait, there was no body, so what were the police investigating?

Where was her sister?

SIX

Not A Dream

At first, Grok thought he was dreaming. On the best of days, his head was a confusing place to live. After spending the night on the neighbor's roof, he was stiff and grumpy, and he knew this wouldn't be a good day.

He blinked. No, not a dream. There was a human sleeping outside his house. He had learned that most humans prefer to sleep inside. As did he, leaving outdoor naps for when a ray of sunshine hit, or he'd had a substantial meal. His stomach grumbled at the thought of food.

The night had been tedious; humans everywhere in his house, vehicles, loud noises. He hadn't been able to return home and eventually had grown bored watching them. He had fallen asleep before they left.

An obnoxious squirrel woke him this morning and very nearly became his breakfast. Which was a disgusting thought and showed how low he had sunk. He was hungry, irritated from being kept out of his home, and now he appeared to be faced with a clone of his human.

He couldn't believe any of the humans he had met thus far were sophisticated enough to make clones. But here he was, faced with the evidence. Why they thought they could swap his human out for one was beyond understanding. They didn't smell a thing alike. And this one didn't look like a new model. Dark circles under its eyes, shabby clothes, and some weird hat on its head—yet more proof that it was not his human as she hated hats. Did they think he was stupid?

They? Grok wrinkled up his nose. Who was they? The answer was like a shadow in the back of his mind that wouldn't come out and play.

Shaking back the fuzzy edges that threatened to take over, Grok jumped up on the porch's handrail and studied the clone.

It was time to get some answers.

Sitting back on his hunches, he used his tail to balance on the rail. He raised his face to the sun, turning his neck this way and that, enjoying the stretch. Then he looked down and reached a big paw into his water bowl and, careful not to flip it, sent a stream of water across the porch to the woman.

The clone moved. Eyes opened and closed. Perhaps it was not fully charged before being dispatched.

The clone's eyes slowly opened, blinking in the intense bright morning light.

Grok sent another stream of water towards it.

The clone scrunched its eyes closed.

Water dripped down its forehead.

"What a weird dream." The clone said.

"Not a dream," Grok replied, knowing it wouldn't understand him.

The clone seemed incapacitated, so Grok decided it was time for a closer look. While its eyes were shut, he jumped from the railing to the arm of the loveseat. Timed perfectly with the sway of the rockers, he padded along the back and crouched low, leaning close to its face.

It was lying in a nest, not at all like the bed his human used, and a book lay across its chest. Grok's eyes narrowed. That was his human's book. She used it to write information about her cases. Human minds were ridiculously simple in their inability to retain everything they needed to know. In the fuzzy parts of his mind, it occurred to him that it was suspicious his human hadn't taken the book with her, yet another thing she had left behind on this most recent trip. But the puzzle, for now, was why the clone would be interested in the book.

"Has to be a dream, a terrible dream. Not going to work today." The clone mumbled and snuggled deeper into the nest.

Grok studied its face. They had done a remarkable job. It was almost identical to his human, but close-up now, he could see the lack of lines around the eyes, and it was missing the extra furrows in the forehead. This clone was softer, with extra bits of fat around the middle and on the face and not as much muscle.

He reached out a paw and slapped the clone.

There was a squawk.

Suddenly, the clone sat up, sending the loveseat rocking.

Not expecting the action, Grok braced and attempted to counterbalance as the bench swung back.

Limbs flailing, claws scrambling, fur flying, Grok fell.

He just managed to get his feet under him as he landed with a thud and found himself nose-to-nose with the clone. Its eyes were enormous as it blinked at him.

"Ho, you gave me a start, big guy." The clone sank back, hand to its chest.

For just a brief second, Grok thought about retreating. But something of the predator in him took over. He loved having his prey at his mercy. He crouched on the balls of his feet and then stalked up its chest.

"Ouch, you are huge! What are you, a Maine Coon? Ugh, you've got to be at least 35 pounds. Can you get off my boob?" The clone clutched at his paw, moving it.

Grok permitted the action, mesmerized by its voice. They had gotten something right in the cloning process.

He settled onto its chest, making sure to be uncomfortably close to cause extra unease, and studied it.

His tactic worked. The clone was already showing signs of stress.

"Hello, I'm Amanda. Are you Alexandra's cat?" The clone tugged nervously at its hat as it tried to engage him.

Grok snorted at the ludicrousness of the ownership claim.

The clone tried again. "Alexandra is my twin sister. Does she live here with you?"

A sister?

Not a clone.

Grok swished his tail.

The sister, Amanda, must have taken that as a yes and, feeling the effects of his interrogation techniques, spilled the information he wanted.

"Something awful happened here yesterday. Well, it happened in the house and my van. Someone died. I've never seen a body before. It really shook me up. So, I had to sleep on the porch." Amanda paused and added. "I hope that was okay."

Grok was satisfied with the truthfulness of her statement and rewarded her by rubbing a furry side across Amanda's wet face.

Spitting out a mouthful of hair, Amanda struggled to sit up as Grok jumped to the porch chair and posed at his full sitting height.

The woman was glancing around now. It was later in the morning, neighbors were leaving their houses, and vehicles were on the road.

Amanda appeared self-conscious about her nest and was trying to tidy the space when her stomach loudly grumbled.

Grok gave a chirp. This was good news. If she was hungry, she would probably feed him, too. He wouldn't have to go hunting.

"Oh, what's that?" Amanda pointed to a basket on the front step.

Grok hissed. That hadn't been there last night, and only his distraction with the clone, sister, this morning would cause him to miss it. He didn't like when he made mistakes.

As the woman lifted the basket onto the table, she asked, "I don't suppose this came from you?"

Grok hissed again.

"Maybe it's a welcome basket from one of the neighbors. That would be very kind since I woke them up last night with police sirens." The human sorted through the basket. "This is an odd gift box. A can of sardines, a screwdriver, rubber bands, plastic cups." She screwed up her face and pulled something out of the basket and put it on the back of the table. "A half-eaten jar of olives? Oh, but this mushroom tart looks delicious. It looks like I have breakfast." Amanda's stomach grumbled again.

She balanced the tart in her hand and settled back down on the loveseat.

Grok studied the basket. This was a strange gift. He had only lived here a year of Earth time, but he had never seen one of the neighbors give baskets like this, except in the holiday season. And the tart didn't smell right. It might have been the disgusting mushrooms. If humans had his sense of smell, they wouldn't eat them. Grok's senses were more finely tuned, and he could discern not only the ingredients but also the malintent of the baker and the gifter that lingered on the basket and tart. It raised his suspicions.

Amanda had lifted the tart from the pan and was about to take a bite when Grok made up his mind.

Launching himself, he knocked the tart from her hand. It sailed through the air, flipping like a coin, until it landed face down on the steps.

Amanda turned big eyes to Grok. "Did you do that on purpose?"

Grok glared at her.

"I would've given you some. Now you can eat it all."

"I suspect it is poisoned," Grok replied for his own benefit, knowing she wouldn't understand him.

He was shocked when she replied. "Ah, that's right. Mushrooms are poisonous for cats. All right, all right, you can have the fish." Amanda stomped over to the basket and pulled out the tin. She popped the top and put the can on the railing.

Never one to say no to food, Grok dismissed his suspicion that this "twin" might also be able to understand him and raced across the rail to the fish.

SEVEN

Cat-accident

Amanda stood and studied the ginormous grey cat gobbling up the fish. He was beautiful—long white hair with light gray stripes, tall ear tufts, and a thick white neck mane.

A drop of water dripped down her forehead and slid into her ear. She swiped it away—then patted her head.

Why was she wearing a hat? Then she remembered the night before and sank back onto the loveseat with a groan.

Last night, after the officers left for the second time, Amanda decided there was no way she could sleep in her van until it had a thorough scrubbing. She'd grabbed her sleeping bag and a couple of blankets and bunked on the wicker loveseat on Alexandra's porch. It was freezing, so she'd pulled on the hat she'd picked up from her sister's entry table, an arty hand-knit cap in swirls of pink and green, to keep warm. She had fallen asleep reading her sister's notebook.

Amanda studied the cat while she tried to figure out

what to do now she was awake. The cat ignored her until the last morsel of fish had been licked clean of the tin. Then it sat back and lifted a paw and commenced cleaning its face. His vivid blue eyes stared unblinking into Amanda's as he studied her back.

She had never gotten an insecurity complex from a pet before. But she had never seen a cat as big or as intense as this one. Finishing its bath, the cat posed regally, like a Sphinx. Feeling self-conscious, Amanda averted her gaze to the unappetizing pile of goo on the steps. Had the cat really said it was poisonous? Had the cat really spoken to her? No, that was impossible.

The fantastical thought was interrupted by a curt female voice. "Alexandra. Have you seen Vik?"

An angry-looking woman with long dark hair leaned a hip against the front fence. She had on white jeans and as she pushed the sleeves of her rose-colored jacket up, several diamond bracelets sparkled.

"No, I'm not—" Amanda's response was cut off.

"Look, I don't have time for games. I just got back into town, and I can't find Vik anywhere. He isn't responding to his cell. Just tell him to call me when you —" She raised a manicured brow with an insinuating sneer "—see him."

The cat growled and leapt off the chair, stalking towards the woman.

The woman pushed off the fence with her hip, then froze when she saw the dropped tart.

"Cat-accident," explained Amanda.

At the woman's scowl Amanda jumped up. "I'm sorry.

Was that from you? Did you bring us the welcome basket?"

Stepping back on her high-heeled sandals, the woman said, "I have no idea what you're talking about. I've been gone all week. Just got back this morning." She gave Amanda a bitter smile. "Why are you sleeping on your porch? Lock yourself out?"

"Oh, no, I'm not Alexandra. I'm her twin sister Amanda."

A suspicious glare was replaced with a look of shock when Amanda swept the hat off her head and ran a hand through her curly hair, now flattened in places.

The woman didn't hide her bold inspection as Amanda rooted in her hair for the tie that held it in its usual bun. Pulling the band free, curly red hair cascaded past her shoulders and into her face. Amanda ruffled it, trying to wake up.

"You really aren't Alexandra?" She raised a brow with an enigmatic expression on her face.

Amanda shook her head. "Did you come to see my sister?"

The woman recovered her poise and laughed, an unsettling sound. "I was passing by on my way home and saw you out here. I stopped to see if you knew where Vik was. But you don't know who that is, do you?"

Amanda shook her head.

"Viktor is my husband, and I'm Sally. I've been out of town visiting our children in LA, but he stayed home this week to go mushroom foraging with his buddies. He should be back, but I can't find him." She tilted her head at Amanda. "Why are you sleeping out here? Didn't Alexandra let you in?"

"Oh, um, no. Funny story. I didn't let her know I was coming for a visit, and she doesn't seem to be here."

"Well, no bother. Vik has a key. When I find him, I'll send him over with it, he knows the way." While her words were friendly, the tone had an edge that made Amanda uncomfortable.

"I'm not sure I'm staying. Thank you, though." Amanda didn't want to admit she had been told to leave by the Chief of Police.

"Well, you should. I'm sure your sister is looking forward to a good long visit. I've got to go unpack. Nice hat." Sally narrowed her eyes at the knit cap in Amanda's hand.

"Oh, I got it from the house," Amanda explained, then realized she had just told the woman she couldn't get into the house. It sounded like she was lying. She should explain.

But the woman was staring off at the neighbor's house, and before Amanda could say anything, Sally turned abruptly and left.

Amanda watched her go. She didn't even know where Vik and Sally's house was, so if she did want to be let in, she would be out of luck. But it didn't matter. The police chief was very clear. Amanda had to figure out how to get the Pink Pup moving again.

A chirping sound came from the cat, who leaped back onto the chair and started grooming.

"You know, cat, what I need are clients, fast." Amanda's brow wrinkled as she studied the plastic plants that Alexandra kept scattered around the porch. "I wonder if there are any pet stores here where I can put out business cards." Amanda searched the blankets for her phone. Finding it, she slumped back on the loveseat.

The phone battery was low, but she had enough. She pulled up a browser. A request popped on her screen to join "Diamond Boots McGee Network."

"Hello! What's this!" Amanda sat up. "Cat! It's my sister's code name!"

The cat tilted his head as if interested, so Amanda explained. "It was this thing our favorite author did, where you made up a code name for yourself based on your favorite accessory and the street you grew up on. I was Butterfly Wings McGee, and she was Diamond Boots McGee. Did she use Diamond's favorite saying as her password?" Amanda read aloud as she typed in "balderdash" in all lowercase.

A new message popped up. "Password accepted. You now have access to the cloud network." A slew of images crossed her screen just as the phone rang.

Amanda let out a startled scream, and the device jumped in her hands. She scrambled to catch it and, flipping over the phone, studied the number. It was the Ocean Wood Police Department. They probably wanted to make sure she was leaving. Amanda braced herself as she answered. "Hello?"

"This is Detective Kim from the Ocean Wood Police Department. We wondered if you could come to the station this morning and identify a body."

Dread washed through every cell in Amanda's body. "Is it my sister?"

"No." He rushed to reassure her. "I'm so sorry. That isn't what I meant to imply."

Relief dropped Amanda to her knees. Her hearing buzzed out. She felt the gentle swish of the cat's tail across her back as her hearing returned.

"We've found the body of a man, and we'd like you to tell us if it was who you saw last night."

EIGHT

Welcome

G rok didn't like this.

He hadn't heard what was said on the phone, but when the sister, Amanda, grew alarmed and asked if it was Alexandra's body, he growled.

He watched the sister sink back into the nest, her face slack as she said, "Yes, please, a car would be helpful." After she finished the conversation, she started a complicated grooming routine.

If the caller was sending a vehicle, it must have had something to do with the body Amanda claimed to have found. With all the people invading his territory last night, he never saw a body. But then he had fallen asleep staring at the stars, unforgivably muffing up his guard duties.

He would make up for it today by accompanying her wherever she went and finding out what was happening.

Soon, a police car pulled up front. The sister, Amanda, he reminded himself, hurriedly finished grooming, pulling her hair up onto her head like a fluffy red fountain, and hurried out to the street. Grok followed, staying in the shadows. An officer of the law with an enormous blonde puff of hair above his lip got out of the car and Amanda started softly humming music. She stared at the shiny rectangle on his chest. "Hi, Officer Hartman. Thank you for the ride."

The male human, the "man" as Alexandra insisted they were called, scowled and opened the car door.

"Don't I get to ride up front?" Amanda's smile faded, and she shuffled from foot to foot.

The officer didn't move.

"I feel like a perp," Amanda muttered as she slid into the car.

Grok jumped in beside her.

"No way. Out." The officer demanded.

The car stank of cleanser and human waste. Grok gagged but didn't move.

When Amanda tried to shoo him out, he dug in his claws.

The man, Officer Hartman, leaned in and grabbed for Grok. He was met with razor-sharp claws and jerked back howling. Wisely retreating, he slammed the door, saying, "Fine. Damages are your responsibility."

As the vehicle moved, Grok gave a satisfied purr and settled in the middle of the seat to clean his weapons.

Worse things than a smelly car and a bad attitude have tried to keep me from my goals and failed. I could reach between these bars and have you at my mercy in seconds. Grok thought as he eyed the metal bars between him and the hairy lipped male.

Grok knew Amanda, who was scrunched up next to a barred window and staring at him with wide eyes, was appreciative of his defense.

In no time, the car stopped.

Amanda jumped out as soon as the door opened. Grok followed more leisurely until the officer tried to slam the door on his tail and received a hiss and another look at Grok's claws.

Grumbling, the officer led Grok and Amanda into the back of a single-story red brick building.

As Amanda followed the grumpy officer into the back of the police station, Grok trailing behind her, all she could think was that she had made a mistake. She shouldn't have come to California to surprise her sister. She should have called or emailed, except she didn't have a phone number or an email for Alexandra. She should have had a backup plan. A place to stay. Now, all she wanted was to make enough money to fill up the Pink Pup's gas tank and get out of town before she was kicked out. She could leave her phone number with a neighbor, maybe the dark-haired woman she had met this morning, and Alexandra would call if she wanted to restart contact with her.

Yes, that would have been a great plan. If only she hadn't found a body last night.

Hartman made several turns through a series of very

beige hallways, slowing when they reached a set of double metal doors. There was a loud discussion and what sounded like pots and pans banging around on the other side.

Beside her, Grok growled. Amanda stopped at the threshold. The officer ignored the warning and pushed into a white-tiled room with a blue epoxy floor. Multiple doors led off on both sides of the room, and a stainless-steel table on wheels docked to a double sink in the back. Amanda could tell from the shape that a body was under the tablecloth.

"Out!" A man's deep voice commanded from the other room.

Amanda backed rapidly out of the room, holding the door for the officer, who ignored her gesture.

Hartman stood his ground. "We're here to look at the body."

"So, go to the viewing room and tell us you are there. You never come in here without authorization." The man instructed, still not appearing.

"This is a police investigation. You can't tell me what I can and can't do." Officer Hartman's face was red as he squared his stance to a defensive position.

The owner of the voice stepped out of one of the side doors. He was covered head to toe with scrubs, a gown, boot covers, a mask, and gloves. Though not much taller than Amanda, he stormed towards them and drove Officer Hartman out of the room.

The gowned man followed and pulled off his mask.

"You can't keep us out. The chief wants her to look at the body."

"And you just bring her in? How long have you been an officer? You know that isn't how you do things. We are collecting evidence in there, and you just contaminated the space. And, what if we were in the middle of an autopsy—you really want her to see that?" His eyes were intense as he stepped closer to the taller officer and stared him down. "You will wait in the viewing room."

"We will just see about that." Officer Hartman stalked off. Amanda was glad to see him go.

"You are humming." The man's deep voice switched from steel to soothing.

"The theme song from this old show about the California Highway Patrol keeps popping into my head whenever I see a police officer here. I can't get it to stop." Amanda felt her cheeks flush at the admission.

The man laughed. Then, as he peeled off his gown, gloves, and mask, throwing them in a medical waste bin, he added, "Well, I'm really sorry about that. It's my first case with this department; they aren't used to working with an examiner. Why, the old coroner was storing food leftovers in the outbound cooler." The man shuddered.

"Eww." Amanda let slip out before she caught herself.

"Right?" He walked over to a sink and thoroughly washed and dried his hands. Then he turned back to Amanda and offered her a hand.

"Ben Reyes. It's my first day as a County Medical Examiner. How am I doing?" He gave a nervous laugh at his joke. It was a warm, deep sound. The man was dressed like Monk and looked like a wild-haired Clark Kent. "They hired my team without telling me. And they've been sitting around for days–they haven't even set up the pathology suite yet. And when I got called in for a suspicious death this morning, imagine my surprise that they had already moved the body. I didn't even get to go to the scene before they released it. It's a complete mess."

When he paused, Amanda thought he was waiting for a response.

"Welcome?" She wasn't sure what to say.

Hands on his hips, Ben paced the hallway outside the autopsy suite. He was about the same as her, 5'9", with another two inches from his dark hair striking out at worrying angles. His eyes were huge behind thick-framed black glasses resting on full, dimpled cheeks.

"Right? Don't get me wrong; I'm happy to be out of San Francisco. And living on the central coast is a dream. But the job turned out to be a little more than I expected. They were just so excited to get another board-certified medical examiner they gave me this whole area to oversee instead of just the one city I'd applied for—which is fine—there isn't a lot of crime here. But we are not set up for a body so soon." He paused in his flood of information and looked back at her.

Amanda nodded and grimaced.

He blinked as he recalled the situation. "Oh gosh. I'm really bad with people. Please. Have a seat."

He jogged over to a chair down the corridor and dragged it back to her.

Amanda flinched as it made a loud screeching sound the entire way down the hall.

"I'm so sorry for your loss. Can I get you something to drink? Were you close? Wait, I shouldn't ask that. How are you doing? Wait, I shouldn't ask that either." He groaned and clutched his hair. "This is why I stayed a forensic pathologist for so long. No people skills."

Amanda smothered a laugh and waved her hand. "I'm fine. I mean, I feel bad, but I don't know the body—the victim—the man." She looked apprehensively at Ben. Had she said the wrong thing? "I'm not very good at this either —it's my first dead person. I don't know who he is. I just found him on the floor of my sister's house yesterday."

"Oh. So, you aren't a relative?"

"No"

"Why did they need you to come down? The responding officer's notes should be sufficient."

"When the officers arrived at the house, the body was gone."

As Ben's eyes widened, she started to explain, but there was a commotion down the hall, and the grumpy Officer Hartman returned with a second man, who he gave a smug smile before saying, "The chief is on her way."

Ben rubbed his hands together and nodded. "Good. I've not yet had a chance to introduce myself yet."

NINE

The Station

The chief arrived with Detective Kim, a big scowl on her face. "What is Grok doing here?" She pointed at the cat.

Amanda straightened from leaning against the hallway wall and looked at the cat sitting in the chair beside her. So, his name was Grok. Amanda couldn't think of a reason her sister would give him such an unusual name. Maybe it meant something to her, like Diamond Boots McGee.

"Mangy old cat almost bit me. Took a swipe at me when I tried to get him out of the car. I'm sure she put him up to it. Goading him on." Officer Hartman pointed to Amanda. Then, he added eagerly, "Want me to call animal control?"

The chief, in formal uniform and black hair tightly wound at the nape of her neck, looked the same this morning as last night, but she sighed wearily. "No. The cat is protective and has good instincts. If he behaves, he can stay." She stared down at Grok as if waiting for his acknowledgment.

It was funny, almost like the cat knew what the chief had said. Grok studied the imposing woman, then nodded, lay down in the chair, and started grooming his face.

Officer Hartman scowled. He then resumed his earlier battle. "This new guy thinks he can run an investigation. Won't let us in to see the body."

Detective Kim, smartly dressed in a blue suit this time, shook his head as the officer spoke. "Come on Hartman, you know that isn't protocol, no matter what the old coroner did."

Officer Hartman tried to respond, but the chief cut him off. "The Medical Examiner is in charge here." She turned to Ben, "Dr. Reyes, so glad to have you on board. You can proceed."

There was a brief pause, where everyone seemed to take a breath before Ben launched into his introductions.

"I'm Dr. Ben Reyes, Medical Examiner of Monterey County. We are still setting up the offices here in Ocean Wood, but we do have the visitor's room ready. If you'll follow me." He moved them down the hall into another room. A huge viewing window with closed curtains lined one wall. Under it, a table with a computer monitor had the city's logo floating around the screen.

Grok followed them into the room and jumped up on the table.

Ben had Amanda take a seat. He sat next to her and typed in a passcode.

"Amanda, I'm going to show you photos of clothing.

Let us know if you recognize them. Take your time." An image of a dark shirt and beige pants, both carefully folded, appeared.

"That could be what he was wearing. I'm sure the shirt was dark blue. And there was something on the pants, a grass stain?" Amanda wasn't sure, but Grok was staring intently at the image on the screen.

Ben pulled up additional photos; the clothes unfolded, and a close-up of the pants zoomed into a green mark.

"Yes. I remember that. But I mostly saw his hands. Do you have a photo I can look at?" Amanda recalled tripping over one of the hands and staring at it in horror. She shivered. "Actually, just the ring. I don't need to see the whole hand. I remember a gold ring with a black stone on his left hand."

Ben glanced over at the detective, who nodded. Ben pulled up another photo: a gold wedding band with a round black opal, the camera capturing the flashes of red within the stone.

"That's it. That was the ring." Amanda sighed. It was all hitting home now. "This was the man. He was dead on the floor in the house when I arrived and then again later in the Pink Pup, my van. The chair! Did you find the chair? It was in the house, I'm sure I passed it. A rolling office chair with yellow cushions. Then I saw him sitting on it in the van."

"Sounds like one of the station's chairs. Like the one that Axel stole when she quit." Hartman whispered, not so quietly, to the younger officer beside him.

"Mrs. Warren, thank you for coming down. We can

take the investigation from here." Detective Kim cut off the comments from the officers as he rose and indicated she should as well.

"Ms. Warren, please, I'm divorced." Amanda felt satisfaction in saying that as she followed the detective back into the hall.

Detective Kim acknowledged her request with a nod. "Give me a minute to talk to the chief, and I'll drive you home."

The detective and chief moved further down the hall and conversed quietly.

The two other officers walked out of the room behind her, their conversation carrying. "The chief should have issued an arrest warrant for her this morning when we found Viktor's body and we couldn't find her."

"Why didn't she?" The younger man asked.

"She's giving her special treatment since they used to be partners, the legendary 'Axel-Rod' team."

"Officers!" Ben emerged from the room and overheard the end of the conversation.

The younger men looked up guiltily at Amanda. Hartman didn't back down. "Well, it's true. Even Detective Kim said the sister should be our main suspect, and no one has even issued an arrest warrant."

The detective and chief spun around when they heard the declaration.

"That is enough." The detective's voice was sharp.

"Officer Hartman, Detective Kim has just started to contact people of interest. But he wanted 48 hours to establish 'probable cause' before issuing a warrant. And your behavior is inappropriate. But since you started it, if you have a problem with how I run things, you know how to contact me or where the HR department is. Understood?" The chief received brisk nods, and both men were dismissed. They hurried down the hall in a squawk of rubber soles.

Chief Rodriquez turned to Amanda. "I want to apologize for doubting your story last night." From the look on the chief's face, the words must have tasted sour. Then she spoiled her apology by adding with narrowed eyes, "You must admit your timing was suspicious."

Amanda wanted to say it was a coincidence, but she doubted the chief didn't believe in those.

"Well, I'm sorry for—" Amanda didn't know what to apologize for. Running out of gas in the driveway? Entering but not breaking into her sister's house? Calling the police when she thought there was a crime. But she suspected her crime happened a long time ago. She didn't know what her sister had told her, but she knew the chief was not her friend. "I'll try to leave as soon as I can."

The chief looked conflicted. "You have two days. Then I want your van mobile and gone from Alexandra's house. It is not unusual for her to drop off the grid for weeks at a time. If you wait in town to see her, you'll have to find a new place to camp."

"Do you know how I can reach her? I don't even have her phone number." Amanda pleaded.

"Alexandra would have given that to you if she had wanted you to have it. And, as you have heard, we aren't having any luck reaching her ourselves." The uniformed woman turned and left without saying goodbye.

"If you can wait a minute, I'll get another officer to give you a ride home." Detective Kim pulled out his phone.

"I can see her home," Ben said.

The detective glanced at Amanda; at her nod, he quickly agreed with the arrangement and left them.

Amanda's stomach growled, and Grok responded with a matching meow, circling her legs.

"That is a strange looking cat. How did you meet him?"

"Yes, he is, and it's a weird story," Amanda said.

"How about you tell me how you met him over breakfast." Ben offered and pointed to the door.

Her stomach growled again, but still, Amanda hesitated; she had no money, and "Didn't you just perform an autopsy?"

"Not yet, just a preliminary review. The postmortem is this afternoon. And I never let work get in the way of food." Ben pats his flat belly. "My treat. I'm new in town and getting to know someone who hasn't lived here all their life would be nice. Besides, I want to hear that weird story. And did you call your van the Pink Pup?" Ben grabbed a jacket on a peg on the wall and started walking down the hall.

Hearing the words breakfast, Grok had already started down the hall.

Amanda hesitated. She had just learned her sister was the main suspect in the suspicious death of a man in her house and would be arrested in 48 hours. Was it true? It had been a long time since she had seen Alexandra. Could she be a murderer? Or had Amanda caused this mess? She had to find Alexandra and do something to help her sister out of this. But what? Amanda rushed to catch up with Ben. Maybe over breakfast, she could figure out what to do next.

TEN

Breakfast

Grok watched Amanda twist her hands under the table as she spoke. "Are you sure you have time for breakfast?"

He thought that was a stupid question to ask. A more important one would be, "*Why was the smartest being in the room under the table?*"

"Oh, yeah. They aren't set up for the autopsy yet, and I need to go to the scene after I drop you off and see if forensics missed anything. Not that they would. I'm sure the inexperienced officer they sent to the scene did a competent job. But I should have been there. I should have been called." As the man, who smelled a cloying combination of lemon and soap, replied, he played with something on the top of the table. Grok heard it thumping as he fumbled with it.

Grok growled. Not only was he relegated to the floor as if some inferior being, like that dog at the next table over who kept sniffing its butt, but he also had to watch the inept awkwardness going on at the table above. Exactly what kind of investigation was this?

"By the scene, you mean where the body was dumped?" Amanda clarified.

Grok's ear popped up. Now, things were getting interesting.

"Yes, the dump scene, not your sister's house. I'm sure Detective Kim is at the house by now." Ben replied.

"He is?" Amanda sounded surprised.

Grok wasn't. Any skilled investigator would want to trace a crime back to where it had occurred. Once Grok had seen the clothing from the body, he knew the victim was the interloping neighbor who had been sneaking into the house whenever Alexandra was gone. If Grok was running the investigation—the edges of Grok's vision grew blurry, and a fuzziness took over his mind.

"Meow." Grok felt weak and stretched out on the floor between the chairs.

Amanda's face appeared. "Hey, big guy! Hang in there. We will get you a second breakfast soon."

Above the table, the Lemon Man, Ben, continued. "Well, sure, now they know you aren't a crackpot, and you really saw a body. They have to treat the house as the original crime scene. That is why they took your van keys, too." He spun something and scrambled after it as it tried to flee the table.

"Crime scene! Was he killed?" Amanda's face vanished from Grok's view as she sat up.

"Uh, I shouldn't have said that." Ben's body had stilled.

Grok, in his nauseous state, could only be grateful. He wanted to examine the memory that had tried to surface but poking at it made him feel worse.

Above the table, Grok heard Amanda starting to connect the dots. "Well, of course, that is why they are looking for Alexandra. Just moving the body would have been enough to make the death suspicious. I hadn't thought it through. I guess it's good I'm not at the house."

"Best to stay out of their way." Ben agreed.

"And you don't have to go?" Grok mused aloud. The man had been going on about being so important to the investigation. Grok was surprised when Amanda repeated his question.

"And you don't have to go?" Amanda paused, "That was weird. I thought I heard—never mind."

"No. Kim is an excellent detective. He won't miss anything."

"And who went to where the body was found?" Amanda asked, and Grok sat up. Amanda was asking the right questions, and when she prodded, it didn't make him feel like his head was drowning in fog.

Under his breath, Ben said, "Let's just say he isn't fond of cats."

Hartman. The fuzzy-lipped man. Grok thought that must have been why he was in the room when Amanda was identifying the clothes.

The waitress set something on the table.

"So, how long have you been in town?" Ben asked.

Grok groaned as the two of them got off the topic of

the investigation and dove back into the land of awkwardness.

"Just got in last night." Amanda sounded like she was still chewing as she spoke.

"You're newer than me. I just started this week, but I'm familiar with the area. My wife and I would take long weekends in Monterey all the time."

He was married? Based on his level of clumsiness, Grok found that unexpected, and from the stillness of Amanda's body, so did she.

A gasp from above proceeded a cascade of condiments off the table. The man, scrambling, grabbed at them, pushing his chair back into a passing waiter loaded with plates.

Grok looked up to see the waiter quickly rebalancing his load until Ben grabbed the tray to help steady it and sent an order of pancakes, skidding across the tables like skipping stones on a lake. One landed in a man's coffee two tables away. He sputtered as the liquid splashed up and soaked his face.

Grok raced across the floor to help clean up the mess while Ben stammered through apologies.

The waiter, a tall, thin man with rolled-up sleeves and a blue apron, did not look impressed, and he sent Ben back to their table.

If Grok hadn't been deep into his fourth silver dollar pancake and wishing for some maple syrup and peanut butter, he would have noticed Amanda grabbing Ben's hand and pulling him into a chair before he could do more damage.

Ben cleared his throat. "So, what was the weird story of meeting Grok?"

Hyperaware of the feel of Ben's fingers against her own, Amanda drew back her hand, and, ignoring the blush that swept up her cheeks, she relayed waking up to the wave of water.

"Grok. It's a strange name, isn't it? You know what it means?" At the shake of her head, Ben continued. "Grok means to understand something intuitively or empathetically. It is not a word I've ever seen used as a name." Ben said to her, then looked down at Grok. "You are a very curious cat."

Grok gave them a sly grin.

A waitress in a blue apron arrived and, pushing the toast plates to the side, safely deposited the remainder of their breakfasts on the table. Ben shoveled most of his eggs and a small piece of bacon onto a saucer and slid it under the table to the cat, "here you go, buddy."

Amanda found it endearing and tried to suppress a smile as she forced herself to eat slowly and enjoy the moment. It had been weeks since she'd had a meal that didn't come in a wrapper, and she felt like she had forgotten all her table manners.

They chatted about the area and their work and

somehow completed breakfast without dropping anything.

Grok didn't look impressed.

As they got up to leave, Amanda groaned and patted her belly; she would be dozing now if she hadn't had two cappuccinos with her waffles and eggs. "Thank you so much for breakfast."

"So, what will you do now?" Ben asked as he paid the bill, leaving a hefty tip to cover the mess.

Amanda thought about Ben's question as she stepped onto the sidewalk in front of the shop and stopped by a sandwich board that read "Monarch Deli & Café."

The sky was white, the thick cloud cover blocking the sun. She shivered at the crisp breeze. California was cooler than she had expected. Where was all the sun and surf?

The one and two-story shops lining the street were busy with shoppers. A young family with a stroller wove in and out of the tables set up in front of the restaurant. An older woman in a quilted vest walked by with a dog wearing an identical bobbed haircut. A car slowly cruised by, looking for a spot in the parking strip that ran down the center of the wide road. Surely, some of these people would need a dog groomer.

"I don't know. It's strange my sister would disappear as a body was found at her house. I want to find her before they have to issue an arrest warrant. I'm worried about her and about what really happened to Viktor. Hey—I just remembered, a woman, Sally, came by this morning looking for her husband Viktor. Is that him?" Amanda asked.

Ben choked beside her. "Uh, can you pretend you don't know that name? And maybe don't say anything to anyone about it until Detective Kim speaks to them? He is taking care of that this morning."

Amanda gave a grim nod and then added. "Since the chief has given me 48 hours to leave Alexandra's driveway, I need to focus on finding grooming clients so I can buy gas and at least have options."

"Well, I can help with that. Qbert won't be happy, but he could really use a bath, and with the move from San Francisco, I've not had time to get him properly groomed in a while. Do you think you could work on him this afternoon? I could drop him by your van."

Amanda was speechless. "Of course. I'm happy to help." She was giddy at the idea of her first client.

"Ah, you say that now. Qbert is an English Sheepdog, and it's been a while since his last bath. My wife used to take care of him. Since she died, I've let a few things slip."

Something made Amanda reach out and squeeze his hand. She quickly released it. "I look forward to working on him."

Ben gave a sad nod.

A phone buzzed in Ben's pocket, and he pulled it out and read the text. Then he turned to Amanda. "Well, they are still setting up the autopsy room, but the police have released the scene where the body was found. I will head over there after I drop you off and take a look. It helps me with the context."

"Do you think I could go to?" Amanda scrunched up her face as she made the strange request, then hurried to explain. "I don't want to turn up at the house while the police are still there. And I'm trying to wrap my head around how he got from my sister's house, to my van, and then to this other location. Maybe seeing the scene would help explain what happened." Knowing the police now believed her didn't erase the self-doubt that had crept in.

"Okay. What they don't know probably won't kill them?" At Amanda's stricken look, Ben apologized, "I'm joking, so sorry—pathologist humor. The scene has been released. It wasn't a crime scene, just a dump. Anyone can go there if they know where it is."

Amanda gave his Ben an uneasy smile.

The Scene

They picked up Ben's car at the station, a serviceable-looking black SUV, and drove down Cypress Avenue, through the town center, and deep into a residential area. Amanda recognized the street Alexandra lived on. They passed a bright green golf course, a community center, and many low, one-story wood buildings. The trees weren't thick like they were in Ohio. They were spars, bare trunks with tuffs of leaves, like clouds at the top, making the trees look taller and more solemn in their isolation. Squat bushes and weedy grass gave way to succulents and sand.

Within minutes, they were almost to the ocean. Amanda glimpsed crashing waves around a corner before they turned down a side road.

Ben pulled over on an empty stretch of road with no houses. Up ahead was a turn into some type of park.

The minute they arrived on the scene, Grok leaped

from the vehicle and nose to the ground followed a smell. Amanda would compare him to a dog who had caught the scent, but she didn't have to say it out loud to know it would probably be hissed at. "Where are we?"

"Just up from Asilomar State Beach. There is a conference center here, beautiful but surprisingly isolated. The detective says employee parking is down this road. The body and chair were found here. Dumped, like it was an accident. There was little evidence from the scene except the location."

"So, there was a chair! I knew it."

Last night had been confusing. Amanda had been so tense at the prospect of meeting her sister and then finding a body that disappeared twice, and no one believed her. It had her doubting herself.

Grok padded ahead of them on the paved road, sniffing the air. The cat stopped directly across from the turn and gave a tail swish.

Ben followed Grok, leaving the road and heading for a break in the dried grass. Crouching down, he examined the ground.

"Good spotting, Grok." The man commended and reached out, hesitant as if asking for permission. The cat leaned into the hand, and Ben rubbed behind the ears and into the scruffy mane while Grok purred.

"Why is the location important?"

"Well, it wasn't concealed. It's possible that whoever transported the body might not have known it was there. They would have to be coming from this direction," He pointed the way they had come. "And it fell out of their vehicle when they went around this corner."

"How could they not know?" Amanda scratched at her ponytail.

"Maybe someone put the body in the back of a delivery truck and when the truck took this sharp corner, it fell out?" Ben tracked Grok, who was pacing in a circle. "They didn't attempt to conceal it. That makes us think they didn't know it was there."

"So, whoever did it was staying here for a conference?" Amanda followed Ben.

"Kim checked. There are no conferences this week, but they might have been staying here. Rooms can be booked by the night."

Grok and Amanda stopped by the road. Ben continued to walk around the scene, taking measurements and snapping photos on his phone. He paced out the distance from the corner to the drop. Then he checked out the road for tire tracks.

Amanda watched, fascinated.

Grok got bored and gave himself a bath.

"Find anything?"

"Well, not so much found, but if my measurements are right, someone would have to come around this corner fast from that direction for the body to land where it did." He pointed down Asilomar Avenue.

"Late for work?"

"Possibly." Ben smiled.

"What?"

"You saw the body about 11 PM. And I'll know the time of death. It shouldn't be a problem to find out what shift they were on and who arrived late."

Amanda grinned, too.

TWELVE

The House

Ben dropped Amanda and Grok at her sister's house with a promise to return later with his dog, Qbert.

The police were gone, and Amanda stood at the foot of the drive and got her first decent look at the place in the light.

The house needed a paint job. Well, half of it. In daylight, it was evident that the house was mid-way through repair. One side a sunny yellow, the other a faded and cracked dirty white. Scaffolding ran up on one side of the place where half the windows were new. The other had boards covering several missing glass panes. The front door needed painting, but the steps and porch floor were new.

Amanda looked closer at the swept-clean steps.

The police must have cleaned up the mess from the dropped tart, or an animal had eaten it. But where was the pie tin? The basket? Even the empty sardine tin was gone.

Had her sister returned?

Amanda ran up the steps. A wide yellow sash of crime

scene tape covered the front door. She hesitated, then knocked. She had a moment of dread that the door would push open. She tried the knob and was relieved that it was still firmly locked. She knocked again. Silence.

Of course, the police wouldn't leave the tape up and then let someone into the house. But she had hoped. Disappointed, she stepped back and studied the cozy porch. Her sleeping bag and pillow were in a pile on the loveseat. Nothing seemed out of place from this morning.

How had Viktor gotten into the house? Did he use his key and then leave the door open? What if he hadn't been alone? What if the person who killed him had broken in and lay in wait?

She should check the outside of the whole house.

"Grok, I'm walking the perimeter. Want to come?" Amanda asked hopefully.

Curled on the chair next to the loveseat with a view of the street and side yard, Grok didn't move; he just watched Amanda with a lazy lack of concern.

So, Amanda slowly walked the outside of the house on her own, looking in every window. There were no signs of damage other than the obvious construction issues. But the ground beneath the windows was covered in footprints. The police must have already thought of this.

Through the windows, Amanda could see the interior of the house. The walls were painted warm colors and decorated with prints. The comfortable furniture and solid wood tables crowded into the small rooms, making them welcoming. It looked like a lived-in, well-loved home, except for the little cones with numbers on them spread throughout the house and the dusting of black powder around the door frames. But Amanda was glad to see the police taking this seriously.

In the backyard, Amanda could see the back neighbor had a huge home that stretched the width of Alexandra's house and the houses on either side. Standing on her tiptoes, she could see all the backyards were small, narrow strips of land divided by tall wooden privacy fences.

Alexandra's backyard had a heat lamp hovering over a weathered oval table and six chairs surrounded by large round planters. In the light, Amanda could see a few plastic leaves, but mostly dead plants sticking out of the tops of the pots and in the raised vegetable beds. The carnage represented more than just a few days of neglect.

It would be safe to say her sister did not have a green thumb. A tree in one corner, behind the shed, had managed to survive, but that might be despite her sister's care.

Amanda turned her attention back to the house.

A sunroom spanned the full width of the back of the house. Between the wall of windows and patio door and the skylights above, the room was brightly lit despite the overcast sky. There were two big puffy reading chairs, a crafts table, and a bookcase covering every wall space without windows. If there was ever sun here, it would be a wonderful place to spend the afternoon with a book. An interior door stood ajar, and Amanda could see a laundry room.

Further down, through a window on the side, she could see into a kitchen with cleared counters. The remaining windows on the far side of the house, away from the driveway, were tightly shuttered. And that was it. Nothing in the space looked like it was waiting for the owner to return, and from the outside, she could find no clues to her sister's disappearance. She hadn't expected to find anything, but she had hoped. Maybe the chief was right, and it was normal for her sister to disappear.

But why leave Grok behind?

"By the way, thanks for the help," Amanda muttered to the cat as she returned to the front porch.

Leaning over the sleeping bag on the loveseat, Amanda started to roll it up. Something hard stuck out of the side, and she fished inside and pulled out Alexandra's notebook. She had only gotten a few pages into it last night before falling asleep. She had read enough to know that Alexandra was a private investigator. This was her current casebook and she was working on four active cases.

Her fingers itched to dig into the book for answers. Why had her sister left the force? How long had she been an investigator? Was she really missing or off on a case? But There was no time now to read. The van had to be prepped for the afternoon client. She tucked the casebook under her arm and rerolled the sleeping bag.

Turning to face the driveway, she hunted inside herself for courage and came up empty. Sighing, she realized determination and a lack of choice would have to do. She could do this.

"Don't mind me. I can handle it." Amanda called to Grok.

The cat ignored her.

The Pink Pup had made it to the end of the gravel drive, which stretched alongside the house and ended in an old shed that a strong wind would demolish.

Amanda patted one of the floppy pink ears on the van as she passed it. Then she opened the front passenger door, tossing her sleeping bag and the casebook inside. Best to have her hands free for this next part.

She shut the passenger door and studied the van. The hot pink wrap made the van look like an enormous cartoon dog. The feet crouched up by the wheel wells, and the giant black nose stretched across the hood. The floppy ears were an after-market add-on her ex insisted on. Amanda hated them. They scared the dogs and created a lot of wind resistance when she drove.

She didn't like many things about her choices with her ex. The worst was picking him over her sister. But she had also dropped her own degree to groom dogs and put him through veterinary school—for the good of the family. And worked for free at his veterinary clinic—for the good of his practice. But the one good choice she had made when they split last year, was getting the van, free and clear, while he got the debt-ridden practice, house and their meager savings account. It had helped her escape.

And now, it had dead body cooties all over it, and it was time to clean it up.

THIRTEEN

Weird Things Humans Do

Grok decided to call this day "Weird Things Humans Do" day. It was a bit long, but he liked the flow. The clone misidentification this morning was funny. Without that hat, it would have been obvious she wasn't Alexandra. And then that ridiculous excuse of an authority figure with the hairy lip, thinking he could play. Grok should have split him in half with a claw. And then the painfully awkward flirting at breakfast, though it did result in some tasty pancakes. However, the neighbor getting himself killed in Alexandra's house was the weirdest.

Grok frowned as Amanda found a hose and attempted to drown her vehicle. Mounds of suds were emerging in waves and flooding the driveway. Every so often, she would emerge from the van, shudder and say, "Dead body cooties," then go back to scrubbing again. However, a commitment to cleanliness was an admirable trait in any species. Of course, nothing was going to completely remove the stench of the dead human's mating scent, part the emotional malcontent, and part a chemical application. It smelled like an old spice mixed with obsession. One of the advantages Grok had was a special organ in his mouth that allowed him to process smells a thousand times more accurately than humans. Probably better than dogs, but he wasn't willing to waste the time to find out. He had told Alexandra for weeks that people were coming into the house while they were gone. That's why she had left him behind on this trip, to guard the house, and—he couldn't remember the other reason.

A low growl rumbled up his throat.

This memory dysfunction felt artificial to his nature and so very frustrating. And since his blunder last night, falling asleep looking at the stars and missing the murder, he was determined to make amends. Alexandra had been good to him, trying to help him recall who he was. His mysterious identity felt like it was on the tip of his temporal lobe, but like prey hidden from predators, it refused to reveal itself.

Was that why he couldn't remember? A protective instinct against a threat? He had assumed he had hit his head during one of the endless training exercises they put him through. *They?* Who was they?

Think! Grok pushed himself to remember even as his vision swamped with grey fog, and he lost consciousness.

Amanda loved her van. And she would love it more when she could comfortably touch it and not feel like she was touching dead body cooties.

Carefully walking across the wet floor, she used towels to push out most of the water. She returned everything to its proper place, wiping dry the surfaces she would need to work on and turned on the dehumidifier. She hummed as she pulled out her favorite shampoo and clippers and set out a fresh set of towels.

After Amanda turned on the generator to heat the water, she slid through the tiny door between the work area and the cab to stash her personal items in the front of the cab and plug in her phone to charge while she worked.

A vehicle pulled up outside. Amanda stepped out to greet them.

Ben parked and was opening the side door of his SUV when the door flew open, and a giant white and grey ball of fur barreled her way.

"Qbert, stop!" Ben hollered.

Before she could establish the dog was okay with being touched, he knocked Amanda back onto the wet ground and attacked her with a big pink tongue.

"Ben tried to pull Qbert off. "I'm so sorry. He's not always like this. He was just so excited to ride in the car."

Ben's voice faded away as he struggled to get the dog under control while trying to help her up.

Amanda rolled to a crouch, staying low to the ground. She held out a hand to Qbert, bracing herself for another tongue bath. The dog had more hair than she'd seen in a long time, and this was her business.

The sheepdog started licking her feet, hand, and arm up to her elbow. When he went for her face, Amanda laughed and pushed him back as she got to her feet. "Hi, boy."

Qbert jumped up and down in place. And Amanda could see where he got his name from as all four feet seemed to hover above the ground before landing and bouncing back up again.

"I'm so sorry." Ben tried brushing off her backside. His hand stilled, and he backed away, repeating. "I'm so sorry."

Amanda blushed and laughed it off. "I am okay. Anything special you want done with him?"

Ben looked out of his depth. "Uh, whatever you decide?"

Running a critical eye over Qbert, she took in the mats in his undercoat. This was going to take a couple of hours. Amanda nodded. "Okay, you can leave him here and go back to work."

"Are you sure? He's a handful." Ben tried to straighten his glasses while he struggled with the leash.

"Yeah, I'm sure. Just hold him for a second while I finish setting up." Amanda returned to the van and pulled out a magnetic sign: "Pink Power Wash & Groom. In session. Please do not disturb." Her new contact information was listed below. She put it on the door, covering the phone number to her ex's veterinary clinic, then returned for the dog. "Alright, Qbert, let's get you cleaned up."

FOURTEEN

Qbert's Path

"Well, Qbert, it's just you and me." Amanda helped him into the big stainless-steel tub, clipping his lead in place, and closed the van door. Just in case he tried to make a run for it.

She loved talking to her dogs. They were the best listeners.

Slipping on a mask, Amanda told Qbert her plan for him while brushing the mats out of his coat. A pink tongue sneaked out, giving her a lick as she started his bath. The sheepdog reveled in the attention, though he didn't like the running water.

Amanda's mind wandered as she soaked and rinsed Qbert.

Why would someone move a body around? She knew from Sally that Viktor had a key. Had he known he was dying when he came to the house? There was a mess on the floor, so he must have been alive when he arrived and then gotten sick. Had he been alone? Amanda thought back to last night. She was sure she heard something upstairs when she was in the house. And the door had closed while she was across the street. Had someone else been in the place?

A lot less dirt was coming off Qbert now. She plugged in the recirculating bathing system and gave him another wash.

The man hadn't been big; she could lift him, but it would be a struggle, and she was used to lifting heavy dogs. But if she could do it, so could her sister. Amanda hoped the police didn't think of that. They already thought Alexandra was involved. Maybe they wouldn't arrest her sister if she proved someone else was in the house.

Qbert's water finally ran clean, and she turned off the hose and grabbed a towel. While she vigorously toweled him dry, she asked, "If you were going to murder someone and didn't want to be found out, would you do it at home, or would you take them somewhere else?"

Amanda realized that if the man wasn't alone when he died in the house, then the other person must have moved the body. But why put him in her van? And how did they get him out of her van and over to Asilomar? She needed to find out who was in the house. Could it be her sister? Could she be the murderer?

Qbert gave her hand a little lick.

No. Amanda may not know her sister anymore, but growing up, Alexandra couldn't abide people breaking the rules; that's probably why she became a cop. No way would she believe her sister was a murderer. So, someone else must have known her sister was gone and taken the victim to her house to kill him.

They'd have to know they could get in.

"Qbert, they had to know that Viktor had a key!"

Qbert gave an encouraging whine from underneath the towel. Amanda pushed back his bangs and looked him in the eye. "I think we need to find out who knew about the spare key to the house."

She let go, and the dog gave a vigorous shake.

Amanda pulled a hoodie over Qbert's ears, put on her ear protection, and turned on the dryer.

How could she find out who had a key? She would have to ask the neighbors. They seemed like a nosey bunch. Undoubtedly one of them would know.

Soon, Qbert was dried, brushed, and clipped. Amanda ran a critical eye over her work. She snipped at another strand to even up his little mustache. Two-thirds of the dog lay in piles on the floor. While he was well-loved and cared for, Ben didn't have much time for maintenance. The short pet trim she had given Qbert would give Ben more time before the next appointment was needed. Amanda kicked the hair aside to clear a path and lowered Qbert to the floor.

While he danced around and licked all the surfaces within reach, she gathered the wet towels and fed them through the laundry chute to the basket in the back she knew was already full from cleaning the van. She would need to find a laundromat soon.

Wait a minute. She had seen a washer through the sunroom window. What if she went to the neighbors asking if anyone had a key to let her in to do laundry? It would have to be after they released the house as a crime scene, and she wouldn't need to stay there. The idea of staying in the house where the body had been physically repelled her. And it would get her in trouble with the police chief. But using the laundry would be okay. And a kind neighbor would hopefully understand that, and she would learn who had access to the house.

FIFTEEN

Meet the Neighbors

Qbert was happy to lay on a towel in the sun at the side of the van. He was exhausted from his ordeal, but his coat looked beautiful. Amanda left a bowl of water for him and headed down the driveway. She hadn't made it more than a foot out of the yard before Grok spotted her and quickly caught up, paws padding beside her.

"I'm going to visit the neighbors and ask who had a key." She felt compelled to explain to the cat.

The cat chirped back, almost sounding like he said, "Of course."

She wanted to start with the backyard neighbor first. That should be Dot's house. It was the direction she had pointed last night. They had the best view of Alexandra's house and maybe had seen what happened last night. But she had to walk around the block to get there.

As she rounded the hedge at the end of the drive, she saw a woman standing next to a Mini Cooper car in the driveway of the house next door. The woman's hair was cropped into a pixie cut, swept to one side of her face, and was such a vivid shade of green it looked like it would be visible from space. The neighbor dropped her keys. When she went to pick them up, something fell from her bag and rolled away. She chased after it, dropping her jacket and purse along the way. This must be the woman Colleen that Dot had mentioned last night. Maybe she had been away.

"Hello!" Amanda waved.

The neighbor jumped, and several more items ejected from her bag as she twisted around.

"Sorry, I didn't mean to startle you." Amanda hurried down the sidewalk and crossed into the yard towards the closest item. "Let me help you pick those up."

The green-haired woman blushed. "No. No. I have it." She rushed to beat Amanda to each item, tossing them into her cloth bag.

"It's no problem." Amanda picked up the duct tape and the rolled-up plastic tarp and added them to the bag.

"I can do it." The green-haired woman yanked a ball of heavy twine out of Amanda's hands and backed away. Almost tripping over the bag she had left on the lawn. She quickly added the ball to the bag and picked it up.

Grok observed the interaction with the bored expression cats had mastered long ago.

"So, what was all the commotion at your house last night?" The green-haired woman mustered a polite smile.

"My house?" Amanda paused and then realized what the woman meant. "Oh, no, I'm not Alexandra. I'm her sister, Amanda. I came to Ocean Wood for a visit, but I didn't plan very well, and she doesn't seem to be around." Amanda didn't think that would ever get less awkward to confess.

With a sound of surprise, the woman flicked green bangs out of her eyes and stared intently at Amanda's face. "You're right, you aren't Alexandra. I just saw you with Grok and thought—" her voice faded out.

Yep, never going to get less awkward. Amanda shrugged it off.

"Actually, I didn't plan my trip very well because Alexandra isn't here right now. And, when I arrived at her house last night, I found a body. That's why the police were here."

Colleen dropped her bag, and the contents went flying —again. Her face was pale as she turned to Amanda. "Really? Do the police know what happened to him?"

"I don't know. But they are looking into it."

The woman looked distressed and understandably uncomfortable about learning a body was found next door. Amanda decided to get back to the original topic. "Have you seen my sister?"

Green hair flopped as she shook her head. "No. It's been a couple of days. Do you think she's in trouble?"

That was the question. Amanda hoped not.

"I don't know. We haven't seen each other in a while. This was kind of a surprise visit. Have you lived next to her long?" Amanda forced herself to step back to give the woman more room. Humans were like animals; they didn't like to feel cornered.

"My husband and I moved in a couple of years ago.

Alexandra was already here. We don't know her well, but we see her all the time." The woman started to fidget, and then, as if she suddenly realized something, she made a startled noise. "I forgot to introduce myself. My name is Colleen Cooper."

"Hi, Colleen." Amanda gave a small wave. "So, I hate to ask, but I'm a dog groomer, and I have a bunch of towels I need to wash. My sister has a washing machine in the back. After the police take down the crime scene tape, is there any chance you have a key to her house and would let me in to do laundry? I know it's a huge favor. I understand if you don't think it's a good idea."

Amanda held her breath as she waited.

"Key?" Colleen squeaked. "NO! No key. Nope. Why would I have a key?"

"Oh, okay." Amanda took another step away from the woman until she was next to Grok again. "Well, I'll let you get back to your painting."

A look of confusion crossed Colleen's face. "How did you know I was a painter?"

Amanda pointed to the woman's yoga pants and flowy white blouse covered in paint spatters. Even her mismatched rainboots had paint on them. Colleen laughed; the sound strangled. "Yes! I'm a painter!" She grabbed her bags and practically raced to the house.

Amanda shook her head and turned to Grok. "Do you know what that was about?"

The cat shrugged as if to say, "All humans are weird," and started walking down the sidewalk again.

Amanda had to agree. She turned to follow the cat.

That had not been a good start to her quest. But she learned her sister hadn't been seen for several days. While worrying, it would remove her sister from being a suspect. But if word got out that Amanda was asking questions, it was bound to make the police suspicious and maybe get her kicked out sooner than the 48 hours—she looked at the time on her phone—make that 44 hours that the chief had given her. She needed to be more careful when she talked to the next neighbor.

Fairy Gardens

Amanda followed Lilly Street to the corner of Cypress Avenue, counting the houses. Turning left would take her to the center of the small downtown area where Ben and she had eaten breakfast. She turned right instead. From the map, she knew if she kept walking, she would be at the ocean in about twenty minutes. She hoped to get down there soon as she had only seen the sea from a distance on her drive in and the glimpse this morning when she and Ben went to look at where the body had been dumped.

Amanda took the first right and counted houses until she came to the one directly behind her sister's house. It was a massive, teal-colored Victorian house that took up a lot and a half. Hopefully, this was Dot's house. It was the direction the older woman had pointed last night.

This house had a double driveway and parked on one side was an expensive-looking SUV. Amanda eyed the parking sticker stuck in the windshield for an LA shopping mall dated the 16th. It made her a little sad, she and Alexandra had been born on the 16th of June. As she walked past the vehicle, she glanced in the back and saw a box of kitchen items and a pair of rainbow-colored rain boots splattered with light-colored mud. If everyone had rain boots here, would she need a pair? Just how much rain did this place get?

Amanda held the gate open for Grok, and they walked up the short path. The yard was small. Every inch had been manicured and pruned and nurtured into a miniature oasis. Even the planters had fairy gardens in them. Amanda wandered off the path to examine a potted Bonsai with flowering purple leaves. A miniature house sat on the moss under the branches. A chair in front of the house had a tiny book and reading glasses on its seat. She leaned in for a closer look.

"What do you want?"

Amanda jumped and whirled at the sound of the voice.

"You startled me." Amanda held a hand to her racing heart as the woman she had met on the porch that morning eyed her from the doorway. The woman whose husband, Viktor, she had found dead last night. Did she know yet? Surely the police had been by. "Sally, right? I thought this was Dot's house?"

"Amanda?"

"Yes."

"Oh, I thought you were Alexandra." The woman relaxed a fraction in the doorway, but her posture was still rigid, and her smile forced.

Amanda's phone rang, and she instinctively pulled it out and looked at the number. Then, hit ignore on the call. As the call pushed to voicemail, a series of pictures flowed across the screen. She muttered, "Why am I getting pictures of Alexandra's house?"

When she looked up, Sally was standing right in front of her.

Amanda gasped and took a step back.

"Dot's next door. Why are you talking to her?" Sally leaned in.

From beside Amanda, Grok growled a low warning sound that pushed Sally back.

Nerves skittered down Amanda's spine and activated a jittery monologue.

"I just—I just wanted to ask about a key. I need to do some laundry. I'm a groomer. Dogs. Cats, too, but they don't like it very much. It's not just the water thing. But I've done a few rescues. And sometimes help with flea dips at adoption fairs–but mostly, it is dogs. I did a hamster once. Pretty easy. And a man brought his ferrets in. Had a whole family of them. Usually, people just do the small animal grooming themselves. But dogs! I've done a lot of dogs and—towels! They use a lot of towels. So, I need the laundry. At my sister's house. Do you know who has a key?" Amanda stopped to take a breath.

Sally stared at her like she had lost her mind.

Grok shook his head.

Sally finally broke the prolonged and uncomfortable silence. "This isn't a good time. I received some devastating news when I returned to town this morning."

"Oh, of course, I'm sorry. I'll go. Sorry for bothering you. Thank you for the directions." Amanda was feeling her way along the picket fence behind her. She eyed the gate and wondered if she could run for it or wait until Sally retreated. She didn't have to wait long. The other woman turned on her heel and went back through the front door, slamming it behind her.

"Come on, Grok," Amanda called. But she needn't have bothered. Grok had already leaped up on the fence and over. Amanda grumbled as she walked around to the gate. By the time she turned back down the street the way she had come, the cat had disappeared.

Amanda took a minute to catch her breath. That had been intense. She hadn't known if she should give her condolences. But what if the police hadn't talked to Sally yet, and she was just acting normal grouchy, not widowed grouchy?

She wasn't sure what to do now other than get off Sally's lawn. She was feeling flustered from the encounter and a little tired from skipping lunch. But Dot's house was on her way back to the Pink Pup, and she had thirty minutes before Ben would be back to pick up Qbert.

"Hello there!" Called a voice from the little blue house squeezed in next to Vik and Sally's, the tiny, shaded porch taking up the whole front yard. Dot was sitting next to a man in a wheelchair. Both were drinking from teacups. "Join us!"

SEVENTEEN

Butterflies and Cypress Trees

"What did that evil old bag say to you?" Dot's tone was sincere.

Amanda raised her brows.

"Oh, don't look at me like that. If you knew what we've been through with those people, you'd call her worse."

Dot turned to her husband, and he nodded.

"Sal and Vik have been the worst neighbors. They sucked up all the land around them and kept building on their house until they had this monster structure. Not at all to historical code. Then they built an apartment complex next to them, and the renters have taken up all the parking."

Dot barely took a breath before she continued. "We are on a tiny little half lot, and when we needed to remove a small portion of the fence between our properties to put in a ramp for Albert's wheelchair, they sicced a lawyer on us. We spent thousands of dollars making the front porch wheelchair accessible and had to rip it all up and change the access to the back door." Dot scowled. Her face red as she shook her finger in the direction of Sally and Vik's house.

Amanda gasped. "That's terrible." She guessed that Dot also didn't know that Viktor was dead. Amanda was starting to wish she didn't know herself. When you learned bad things about people after they were dead, you tended to edit your feelings. "Was it just a misunderstanding?"

"Sal does it to be ornery! Vik's just mean. He loves to throw his weight around. Big Deal Vik is blackmailing or bullying everyone into doing what he wants. Oh, and the arguments. All times of the night, yelling and breaking things. I don't blame Sally for spending all her time in Southern California with her kids." Dot shook her head and reached over and patted Albert's hand on the arm of the wheelchair.

"But you showed them." Albert chuckled, turning his hand around to wrap his fingers around Dot's gently.

"What did you do?" Amanda held her breath as she waited for the answer.

Dot blushed. "Oh, it was nothing. Enough about this. How are you getting on?" Dot poured Amanda a cup of tea from the teapot on the table and set it down expectantly in front of the free chair.

Amanda wanted to follow up with more questions. What had Dot done to get even? Could it have caused Vik's death? But it was apparent the topic was closed.

Amanda sat at the table and told Dot and Albert about her first job. They both laughed at Qbert's exploits. As

Dot wiped her eyes, Amanda took a moment to study the couple. They constantly checked in with each other. When one laughed, they turned to each other and shared their joy. And somehow, they were always touching: on their arm, holding hands, Dot's leg brushing Alberts.

They were adorable.

Amanda felt a pang in her heart she recognized as envy. She had always wanted someone to laugh and share with. She'd had it with her sister a long time ago. She'd hoped to have it with her ex-husband. But that wasn't the type of relationship they had.

"Well, now I have a lot of laundry, and I wanted to ask if you had a key to Alexandra's house. If so, could I borrow it to use her washing machine?" Amanda did not mention that any laundry would have to wait until after the police released the house as a crime scene.

"Well, of course, hon, that's not a problem. You can keep the key; now, where would it be?" Dot got up from her chair and went into the house, leaving the bright red door open behind her.

It occurred to Amanda that none of the houses here had door or window screens. But then she hadn't seen a bug since she arrived.

Amanda sat quietly with Albert, sipping her tea. From the way the porch jutted out she could see both up and down Driftwood Drive.

"What are those trees?" She asked Albert, pointing to several large trees on the other side of the street that shaded the porch.

"Cypress. You find them everywhere here. Very hardy

in this environment." Amanda nodded. Then gasped as a butterfly fluttered in and landed briefly on the deck. "A monarch!" She pointed to the brown and orange insect, even though Albert had a clear view.

He laughed. "We get them all the time, especially this time of year. Have you been to the Monarch Grove Sanctuary yet?"

Amanda slapped her hands to her mouth in excitement. "No, where is it?"

"Not too far from here. Mid-October to March is the best time to see them, but you'll see wanderers every so often throughout the year.

The butterfly lifted off the porch and carried on with its erratic path. Amanda's eyes followed it out into the sunshine. "There it goes. I'm glad that fog left. It was cold." She shivered in memory.

Albert laughed. "Don't you worry. It'll be back. You have never been to this area before?" Amanda shook her head, and Albert continued, "This is Ocean Wood. We have fog every morning, every night, and most days. When you see the sun, enjoy it."

Dot came back out of the house, a scowl on her face. "I can't find the key. I don't know where I put it. Albert, do you know where it is?" Her husband shook his head. Dot snapped her fingers, and her shoulders sank. "Oh, I can't bear to think of you sleeping on the porch again."

Amanda waved away her concern. "It's OK. I can sleep in my van. I've been doing it for weeks. But do you happen to know who else might have a key?"

"Well, I know Vik has one, also Frank, Colleen, Anh

and Amy." At Amanda's raised eyebrows, Dot laughed. "I know, that's a lot of people. Alexandra was particular about who had access to her house—it must have been the cop in her— but she was gone for work a lot and she had us look after Grok."

"Grok is an unusual name." Amanda started to ask, but Dot interrupted with a laugh.

"You're telling me. He's notorious in the neighborhood. He has this strange relationship with the Bay Area people's dog and has terrified most of the squirrels and birds. The only animals not afraid of him are the butterflies. Albert kept calling him Gronk, like that football player, until Alexandra corrected him. She is very protective of that cat. Went from super independent a year ago to glued to this cat, almost like he was working cases with her."

"So, everyone knows she is a private detective?" Amanda thought about the casebook in the van that she was itching to read more of.

"Of course. And she is a good one! There was an incident, we don't talk about it, but she saved my skinny little butt." Dot slapped a hand on the aforementioned piece of anatomy. "It is strange she didn't take him this time, especially if she was going camping."

Amanda searched her childhood memories for any camping experiences. When they were young and still had their parents, they had gone a couple of times; sometimes, they even went canoeing and rock climbing. But it had been a long time. Sadness washed over her. "How did you know she was going camping?"

Dot scratched her head and looked at Albert. He shrugged. "I guess I just assumed that's where she went. Unless it was a case."

"I can't imagine it. I guess I don't know her very well anymore. How long has it been since you have seen her?"

Dot patted her hand. Then she scrunched up her face as she thought about Amanda's question. "About a week? Maybe less? You should ask Frank. He keeps an eye on the happenings on Lilly Street. He can see everything from his studio."

Now, that was interesting. Amanda was about to ask more questions when a street commotion distracted them. A pair of police cars arrived and parked in front of Sally and Vik's house.

"What's all that about?" Dot asked, leaning forward. Her eyes were eager.

Detective Kim got out of the first car, and Officer Hartman and his younger partner got out of the second.

Dot and Albert watched with wide eyes as the police opened the gate and walked up to Sally and Vik's front door."

Amanda felt horrible as she explained that Viktor's body was found this morning.

Dot gasped. They watched in astonishment as the officers entered the house. "Oh, poor Sally. What a loss for the neighborhood."

Amanda snuck a peek at Dot, who clucked her tongue and gathered their teacups.

EIGHTEEN

Looking Around

Grok left Amanda before she headed to the short trickster's house. The older woman was okay if you stayed alert, prepared for whatever mischief she thought up. The old man was dangerous, his wheeled vehicle leaving a trail of carnage and broken cat tails.

Once, Grok had eaten a special gummy the man had dropped. Alexandra said he was baked and had to carry him home. He hadn't felt like pastry, more like jelly, loose-limbed, and relaxed in a way he hadn't been since he arrived a year ago—A stab of pain went through his head at the thought, and Grok quickly dropped the memory. Returning his fractured mind to the task, what was Sally up to?

Grok skipped around the house to the apartment complex next door. He took the outside stairs to the second floor, the soft pads of his paws noiseless on the tiles.

Sally told Amanda she had received devastating news. But from the number of fights and the level of malice between the couple, the woman could only be devastated that she hadn't witnessed her partner's demise. A harsh but true assessment, based on the car-sized hole she had once made in the side of the house where her husband had been standing after an argument.

Grok ran along the landing until he was looking over the fence that led to Sally and Viktor Walker's yard. The couple had the tallest fence in the neighborhood. They had also made sure that from nowhere in the apartment building could you look into their yard. Not a courtesy, they offered the rest of their neighbors. Grok had used this vantage point for many hours of spying on his evil nemesis that lived next door.

At the thought of the Bay Area neighbor's dog a growl emitted almost involuntarily. Grok shook it off. Stinky wasn't in town this week, so there would be plenty of time later to mine his yard. Now, he was on a mission.

Grok jumped from the open landing across the gap to the fence. Balancing his large body, he carefully worked his way to the Walker's higher fence. Stopping, he took a moment to steady himself. The risk here was two-fold. If he fell, he would look ridiculous. And Grok didn't like looking the fool. But he could brush it off and try again if he fell outside the fence.

If he fell inside—Grok shuddered.

The Walkers had a shed close to the fence, with a secret gate behind it, but he couldn't open it. And the roof of the shed had been lined with metal spikes. At one point, Sally had installed razor wire, which Alexandra had gotten them to remove. So, Sally started keeping a can of cat mace on hand. He only had to be blasted in the face once to ensure it didn't happen again. Worse than a skunk. One memory he would be happy to forget.

There was a tree at the corner of Alexandra's yard, the branches of which hung over the edge of the Walker's fence, and they had not yet taken a chainsaw to them. He stealthily made his way there.

He could see the authorities talking with Sally Walker from his vantage point. He didn't understand why they weren't tearing the place apart, looking for evidence. Looking for Alexandra.

He scrunched up his nose and tried to pursue a fleeting memory that rippled through his mind...where had she said she was going? He wobbled on his perch and let go of the wayward thought.

At the very least, authorities should be hauling Sally into headquarters and putting her in chains until they had answers. But humans tended to be soft and easily manipulated. And from the tears pouring down Sally's face, she was working these officers over like a pro. They shuffled awkwardly and hurried out as soon as they could.

The second they drove off; it was like a switch flipped in Sally. She stormed the house, ranting and yelling. She pulled clothes from closets pictures off walls, and everything went into boxes, except for the items she burned.

Grok grew bored of watching the chaos. Then he grew hungry. He was just imagining a large pink fish when his attention wandered, and he felt himself slip.

With a thud, he landed in a pot on top of a fake plant in Alexandra's backyard.

NINETEEN

The Studio

Amanda looked at her phone. There was still time before Ben arrived to check out one more neighbor. She got directions from Dot to Anh and Amy Nguyen's house. Walking back up to Cypress Avenue, she turned left and left again until she was back on Lily Street, then headed down the street to the house one over and across from her sister's home.

It was another beautiful Victorian, but nowhere near as big as Sal and Vik's. The one-story house had another one of the rare driveways on the side and was painted two shades of blue with white trim and a light grey picket fence out front.

When Amanda arrived, a man was getting out of a jeep in the driveway. She recognized the fleece jacket.

"Hello, Anh!" She called out, projecting her voice to chase the man trying to disappear through a gate around the side of the house. "Do you have a minute?"

Amanda hesitated, then slid past the jeep and hurried

up the grass and gravel drive to follow the man through the gate. Inside, she stopped. The side yard had piles of cleaning supplies and neatly stacked boxes of automotive parts.

Wait, Amanda tilted her head sideways and read the print on one package. They weren't for a car; they were RV parts.

"What are you doing here?" Anh looked panicked. He searched behind her as if someone else would come through the gate next.

"I'm sorry for intruding. I had a question." Amanda asked.

"What do you want?" He said in the belligerent tone children used when they were caught doing something wrong.

What was he nervous about?

"I just had a question about my sister, Alexandra." She used the tone she reserved for calming dogs and Jack Russell Terriers.

Anh scrunched up his brow and waited for Amanda to continue.

"When was the last time you saw her?"

"Oh, Uh, I don't know. A couple of days or weeks? Maybe. Not sure. We don't talk often. I sometimes see her on the way into the office. She rents a space near our agency. She is busy with her business. And I run a very, very successful travel agency. We are a gold provider of luxury experiences and destinations in Monterey. It keeps me very busy. Very." His voice trailed off. Then he blurted out, "My wife, Amy, would know." But she's not here now. So, you'll have to go away. I mean, come back another time." He made a shooing motion.

It was apparent he was eager to get rid of Amanda. She debated whether to tell him about Vik and then decided it wasn't her place.

As he herded her towards the door, Amanda said, "Do you have a key to my sister's house? I was hoping to do some laundry there." She felt weird every time she asked someone for a key, doubly so when they tried to squeeze her out of a partially closed door. The handle on the gate jabbed her in the ribs as the man advanced.

She pushed through to the other side.

"No!" Anh slammed the door behind her, and Amanda heard a lock clicking into place.

That was weird.

Amanda turned sideways to slide past the jeep in the drive and was relieved to step back on the sidewalk.

"Hello!" A man's voice called. Amanda looked around. No one was there.

"Over here." The voice said.

Amanda followed the sound to the house next door, across from Alexandra's.

The garage door was wide open. She stepped inside. It was a full pottery studio. The man she called Rainbow Crocs was sitting at a pottery wheel with a lump of clay in front of him. "You found me!" He laughed at her expression. "Not what you were expecting, is it?"

Amanda shook her head.

"Well, I find I do my best thinking out here. The house is my husband's domain. But this studio." He raised his arms and waved at everything around him proudly. "This is my Kingdom."

Amanda laughed at Rainbow Crocs' comment, then mentally corrected herself, remembering his name was Frank. Having a friendly neighbor to talk to after the uncomfortable experience next door was a relief. "It's impressive. Have you been throwing pots long?"

"Ever since I retired. I was too stressed at my job. It was bad for my health and bad for my relationships. This is much better." He pounded his fist into the ball of clay on the wheel, flattening it. He patted the mound back into a ball and muttered unconvincingly, "Much better."

"Maybe I shouldn't keep you." Amanda backed away.

"No, no, please don't let me scare you off. As my husband, Bob, will tell you, I did not adapt to retirement easily. It wasn't my choice. But now that I'm here. I'm making the best of it."

"You didn't want to retire?" Amanda leaned on one of the counters, saw all the dust, and pulled away.

"No." Frank took a moment and a deep breath. "My business partner," he emphasized the words as if they tasted foul in his mouth, "decided the business was better without me. So, he squeezed me out of the development company we had spent decades building together." The lump of clay under Frank's hand squished flat again.

"I'm sorry to hear that. It must be hard having such a successful neighbor next door." Amanda said as she brushed clay off her jeans.

Frank tilted his head. "Who?"

"Well, Anh and his wife, Amy. He says his business is

doing really well." Amanda pointed in the direction of their house.

"He said that? Oh, that just made my day." Frank roared with laughter, then clutched his stomach. "Ouch, still sore. I had food poisoning a couple of days ago and can still feel it sometimes. Anyway, Anh and Amy are on the brink of losing their business. That's why Amy is spending so much time working a second job. Their landlord found a loophole in their lease and is kicking them out, and they don't have the money to move. Travel agencies aren't what they used to be."

"I wonder why he lied?" Amanda asked, leaning against a shelving unit.

"No one wants to admit when they're going under. People stop taking your calls. Can't even get the police to respond to calls about a theft." Frank squished the clay flat, then, sighing, grabbed a tool and scraped it off the wheel. "But enough about my troubles. What can I do for you?"

"Please, do you know where my sister is or how I can contact her? I'm really worried." Amanda leaned in, eager for news.

"I'm sorry. I don't. It's only been a couple of days since she left. I'm sure she will be back soon. I don't know who is watching Grok this time. She didn't ask me. But I can give you her phone number. It's probably the one you already have."

"You can? Yes, please!" Amanda felt a rush of joy. She would have her sister's number.

"My phone is in the house. I'll bring it over this

evening once I've cleaned up. How are you doing otherwise?"

Amanda was so excited that she bounced on her toes as she told Frank about her first client and her hope for more work.

While she talked, Frank stood and walked over to a canvas table where he reshaped the clay into a cone before resuming his seat, slapping the clay onto the wheel, and starting it moving.

Do you know who might have a key to my sister's house?" Amanda shook herself to stop staring at the spinning wheel. Something was soothing about it.

"Sure." He listed the same group Dot had. "Do you need a key?"

Amanda nodded.

"It's on the wall. Help yourself." His hands were full of the spinning clay. Frank indicated with his head a series of hooks beside the door.

Amanda studied the keys and selected one that had a feathery cat toy attached to it. It wasn't a very secure location. Anyone who knew it was there could reach in and grab the key. "This it?"

Frank laughed. "Good guess."

Amanda pocketed the key. So, she could access the house now, but so could anyone else who knew where to look.

"Look at that." Frank slowed the wheel to a stop and studied his new pot with pride.

Amanda looked at the sloping, squat cup on the wheel. Was he done with it?

"Ain't she a beauty. Might be my best one yet." Frank swiped a thin wire underneath the pot and gently used his hands to lift the cup and place it on a plasterboard. Rising, he slid the plasterboard onto a shelf behind Amanda that held at least three dozen chunky, crooked cups.

"Lovely." Amanda didn't know what else to say. "I should go. Thank you for everything."

"We neighbors have to stick together. If you need anything while waiting for your sister to return, just let me know. Hold on a sec. I'll walk you out."

They headed to the large rolling garage door, where they had a good view of police cars pulling up in front of Colleen's house.

"I wonder what that's about." Frank's face was puzzled.

"I should probably tell you that the person who died in Alexandra's house was her backyard neighbor Vik." Amanda still wasn't sure if she should be sharing that information.

"Vik?" Frank choked out the name. "That vermin finally got what was coming to him?"

Amanda gasped.

Frank studied his rainbow-colored Crocs and shook his head. "You should probably know. That landlord who was ruining Anh was Vik. And my ex-business partner— that was also Vik. He did a lot of people wrong in this neighborhood."

Amanda was startled by the news. Just who was this Vik that he had hurt so many people? She shifted uncomfortably beside Frank, wondering what to do after a bomb-shell reveal like that. Should she leave? Should she stay?

While she tried to sort out her next move, she and Frank watched silently as the detective knocked on the door, and Colleen answered. Frank and Amanda couldn't hear what the detective said.

Colleen was acting strange. She kept looking behind her and out onto the street and all around as if she was waiting for something, looking for someone.

"What's wrong with her?" Frank asked.

"They must be giving her the news. Was she close to Vik?"

"Well, they dated in high school, but I wouldn't say they're friendly neighbors now." Frank supplied with a shrug.

Amanda was reeling from how tightly connected this community was.

Another car came down the street, and Amanda was relieved to see Ben back to pick up Qbert. She quickly said goodbye and headed across the street.

TWENTY

Pig Reveal

"Ready to See him?" Amanda teased as Ben got out of his car.

"I can't wait."

They walked around the car together and headed up the drive.

Ben stopped. His mouth dropped open. "Qbert?"

The sheepdog leaped up when he saw Ben and started pulling on his leash. Amanda rushed over and released him. Qbert dashed to Ben, jumping up on all four feet. He bounced around Ben in a circle. Ben got down on one knee and rubbed his hand over the dog's side. "Boy, I almost didn't recognize you. You're half the dog you used to be."

Qbert shook his head in glee. He jumped up on two legs, put his front paws on Ben's shoulders, and bathed his face with his tongue. Ben sputtered and pushed back to his feet to escape the barrage. Qbert resumed his dance around Ben.

"Does he look okay?" Amanda held her breath as she waited for the verdict.

"Okay? It's amazing! I forgot what was under all that fur." Ben's huge smile lifted his black-framed glasses on his cheeks.

"Oh, that's a relief. I was worried I had gone too far. But I knew how busy you were, and I thought if he had a great cut now, you wouldn't have to worry about it again for a while." Amanda sagged with relief and leaned against the Pink Pup as she watched Ben play with Qbert. "How was work?"

"Good. We finally have the suite of rooms set up, and I'm training my staff. They might work out." Ben acknowledged her raised brow, "I know they are technically qualified, but I'm not sure about their loyalty and procedural experience. I'd rough it out if it were just one city, but this is the whole area. I need to know they have my back."

Amanda nodded. "That seems fair. Want to come in for coffee?"

"I heard they released the scene. Have you got a key to the house?" Ben asked.

"I have the key, but I actually meant inside the Pink Pup," Amanda patted her van. "When the generator is running, I can make tea and coffee."

"With the scene released, I can take down the tape on the door. The forensic team might have messed it up a little. Let's check it out." Ben tilted his head to the side to study her.

Amanda frowned. The gesture felt familiar. She

glanced down at Qbert. The sheepdog was doing an identical head tilt. She laughed and watched as the dog got distracted and chased after a monarch butterfly. "I'm not sure I should. I feel weird about going into her house."

"Is it the body thing? I can go in with you if it would make you more comfortable." Ben offered.

Amanda thought about it. "Well, yes, the body. But also, my sister doesn't know I'm here, and I'm not sure she would want me in her house. Things weren't good between us when she left Ohio."

"Wasn't that fifteen years ago?" At Amanda's nod, Ben continued, "I never met your sister, but that is a long time to hold a grudge. Were you close before?"

"Very. We had dreams of coming to California and making our mark. Together. I messed it up by chickening out and marrying the wrong man."

Amanda became preoccupied with tracing a seam on the smooth pink wrap that covered the van. She had never forgiven herself for messing up the one perfect thing in her life—her relationship with her sister.

"Well, what would you have done if she had turned up in Ohio?" Ben stepped closer.

Amanda didn't hesitate. "I'd throw my arms around her, apologize, and swear never to make another mistake again."

Ben chuckled. "You'd welcome her? So, why would she do any different for you?"

Amanda hadn't thought about it that way.

Ben glanced around and, seeing he was out of earshot of the police next door, whispered, "Come on. I'll tell you about my autopsy suite while we check out the house." Ben reached out a hand for the key, and Amanda handed it over.

"You have a very strange way of sweet-talking a girl, Ben Reyes."

"Ha!" Ben laughed. "Wait until you hear my poetry."

As Ben headed for the porch, he started reciting a terrible poem that sounded more like a medical examiner's sea shanty.

Amanda groaned, then laughed. "All right, all right. I surrender." Dropping her voice, she asked, "Can you give me any details on the case?"

"Well, I can't tell you much except that you were right about the green stain on his hands. We found it and have it out for analysis. And the chief doesn't think you are a suspect, but she sure doesn't like you."

Amanda grimaced. She climbed the porch steps and stood next to Ben. "Hey, what happened to the tape?"

"An officer must have taken it down already. Where's the key?" Ben held out a hand. Amanda handed it over while he kept talking. "As far as I can tell, the chief is a good officer. And very protective." Ben pushed open the front door and walked into the living room. He stood off to the side, right where the body had been.

The place was a mess. There were dark smudges on the walls and door frames where they tried to get fingerprints. Everything felt askew as if it had been shifted while being searched. Even the pictures hung crooked, and the drawers were slightly open.

Ben spun in a circle. "See, just a house...after a forensic

team has been at it. Let's check the kitchen." Ben opened a door and disappeared inside. A second later, he was back. "That's a closet. I was checking it for you. All clear. Let's try this one instead." He opened another door and entered; when he didn't return immediately, Amanda followed him.

Ben was standing in a moderately sized kitchen that had been recently renovated. New chrome fixtures, modern tile backsplash, and granite counters frame new appliances. "It's beautiful. What a great place for a meal—with a little cleaning. We should turn off the HVAC while here, and if you toss the rug in the living room, I think the rest we can clean ourselves."

Amanda sagged against the counter, then saw the dark dust and recoiled. "Can it be scrubbed off?"

"I'll help you. I have a special vacuum." Ben opened every door in the kitchen until he found the laundry room. "*Voilà.*" He waved his hand like he had magically made the washer appear.

Amanda groaned.

Grok jumped up on the counter and managed to look wholly unimpressed and a little disgusted at the same time.

"So many critics," Ben muttered good-naturedly. He pulled open the fridge. A lone pack of pre-packaged food lay on a shelf. "Okay, so I won't be inviting myself over for dinner. How about I take you out instead?"

Immediately, nerves twisted in Amanda's stomach. That sounded like a date. Was it? Amanda didn't know and didn't trust her judgment with men anymore. Surrounded by graphite powder and a released crime scene, every fiber of her being just wanted to find her sister and be someplace safe.

"I'm going to pass. But thank you." Amanda hoped she hadn't put Ben off entirely because she liked having him around.

"It was the poetry, wasn't it?" Ben shook his head. Then smiled. "Another time."

A hissing sound stilled them both. "What is that?" Eyes wide, Amanda glanced around.

Looking startled, Ben ran to the window. He put his hand to his heart and slumped against the sink. "It's just the outside sprinklers. They must be on a timer."

Suddenly his eyes bulged at something he saw out the window, and he raced back to the front door, yelling, "Qqqqbeeeerrrt, Noooooo!"

Amanda ran to the window in time to see Qbert jump with all four feet into a newly formed puddle beside the front flower bed.

TWENTY-ONE

Identical

Qbert only required a towel dry to resume his previous glory. But Amanda had no doubt he would find something else to get into—and soon. Ben paid her for the grooming and rushed Qbert to the car before he located another puddle.

After Ben left, Amanda stood by the Pink Pup, feeling lost. It still felt strange going into the house. Ben had helped her overcome that initial fear, but it was clear from the chief's dislike of her that Alexandra wouldn't be as welcoming as Ben had implied. Amanda was reluctant to pry any deeper into her sister's private space.

Remembering that her initial goal was to get laundry done, she climbed into the Pink Pup and loaded her laundry baskets. It took several deep breaths to cross the threshold and then more trips to haul all the dirty towels into the house. But her nerves started to settle as she sorted her and put in the first load. The towels would go last since they would take the longest to dry. She decided to start cleaning the kitchen while she waited. Ben had shown her the right cleaner to use on the counters and floors and promised to return with something that would work on the walls. She was filling a bucket with hot water when she got a swipe from a big fat paw.

Grok reached over the counter and stabbed his claws into her, stopping her abruptly.

Amanda yelped.

Grok glared.

"What is your problem?" Amanda asked.

"Hungry." With narrowed eyes, Grok glared at her. Then, he jumped off the counter, walked over to the refrigerator, and put a paw on the door.

Amanda frowned. Did the cat just say he was hungry? Couldn't be. This house was messing with her mind.

She walked over next to Grok, "Is there something in there you want?" Amanda opened the fridge and stuck her head inside.

Grok backed up and sat down on the floor. "Come on, human, good girl. You can do it."

Amanda pulled her head out. "Did you hear that?"

She looked around the empty room and then back at the cat.

Grok looked at her empty hands and sighed, shaking his head.

Amanda leaned back into the fridge and pulled out the only thing inside. She examined the packaged contents and read the label aloud, "Farm Fresh Cat Food. This what you want?" Amanda asked Grok, waving the package.

The cat nodded, turned, and raced to the countertop, jumping up and eagerly waiting for food.

"That's some pretty fancy food you have there. I've never even heard of it before. My sister buys that for you?" Amanda felt a little ridiculous asking the question. Of course, her sister bought it for the cat. Who else would buy it?

Amanda put down the package she had half open. Was there someone else living with her sister? Did she have a partner? Spouse? Roommate? Cat sugar-daddy? Maybe that person went with her. Amanda realized that not only did she not know where her sister was, but she knew very little about her life. She didn't know who Alexandra really was. Would it be so impossible that she could have committed murder and run?

Another swipe of claws had Amanda gasping and resuming her task. "Okay, big guy, I'm doing it." She saw no cat bowls on the floor, so she took a clean saucer from the cupboard and emptied half the container into the bowl.

Grok growled when she leaned down to put the bowl on the floor.

Amanda raised an eyebrow. "You eat on the counter. Really?" She put the bowl on the counter without waiting for a response.

Grok attacked the food like a starving animal. Which she knew wasn't true since the cat had eaten an entire can of sardines, several pancakes, and half of Ben's eggs this morning.

While she was certain Grok could eat the entire

container, she thought it prudent to save a little in case it took a while to find, or afford, replacement food. She folded over the bag and placed it back into the refrigerator. As she closed the door, the gallery of photos held in place with magnets caught her eye. As identical twins, she and Alexandra had always celebrated their likeness. They never dressed the same, but they did have swap days where they would spend the whole day as the other twin and never tell anyone. Not even their family had known. Now, looking at the face that most people would say was identical, Amanda could catalog the differences: deeper lines around the eyes, a small scar near her mouth, and the most obvious, the riot of red curls straightened and cut into a short Pixie style that complemented Alexandra's face.

In one photo, she was canoeing with friends. In another, she was accepting a commendation in her uniform. A third photo showed her parasailing. Amanda was amazed her sister had led such a remarkable life. Citations. Friends. Career success. She had achieved their dream.

Amanda couldn't help the wave of sadness that washed over her. Her life had been so different from her sister's. But she was happy for Alexandra.

Sometime later, somewhere between her second and third load of laundry, Amanda had a big basket of folded towels and was heading out to the Pink Pup to stow them away when there was a knock at the front door.

Grok, who had been sleeping on the couch in the living room, unaffected by the mess around him, jumped up and put himself between Amanda and the door.

Juggling the basket, Amanda reached past the cat and opened the door.

Chief of Police Gina Rodriguez stood on the porch. Her hat was in her hands. Her dark hair was parted and pulled so tightly away from her face that it added to the woman's stoic mask.

"I see you found a key." The chief wasn't asking a question.

Amanda shifted nervously. She stepped out onto the porch, followed by Grok, and sat the basket she was holding down. She would probably need her hands free if she were about to be arrested. "One of the neighbors had a key. I'm just here to do laundry. I'm not staying in the house."

The chief didn't respond.

She wasn't arrested yet, so Amanda continued. "When was the last time you saw my sister?"

"Why?" The uniformed officer's eyes narrowed on her.

"I've been talking to some neighbors, and they mentioned she's been missing for several days. I'm worried about her."

"It's normal for Alexandra to go off camping or follow an investigation for weeks or months without telling anyone. She's very independent. And why were you talking to the neighbors about it?"

Amanda tried to explain her reasoning. "I want to find out who might have had access to the house; surely whoever killed that poor man had a key to get in. I didn't see any signs of a break-in."

Surprised crossed Chief Rodriguez's face. "You need to

stay out of it. This is a police investigation. We don't want you confusing witnesses or contaminating evidence. We cleared the house. You clearly have access. I'm not going to stop you from entering. But you will be arrested if you interfere."

Grok growled low in his throat, and the chief glared at him.

Amanda thought she would be relieved when the chief finally showed some emotion, but she found her legs shaking instead.

"Hey, Amanda!" Frank loped across the street, his plastic shoes slapping the pavement. "Here is Alexandra's phone number." As Frank drew near, he smiled at the chief and then handed a piece of paper to Amanda.

Excitement buzzed through her as she clutched the paper to her chest. "Thank you so much!"

Frank gave a mock salute to Chief Rodriquez, "Ma'am, thank you for your service."

"It wasn't a break-in." The uniformed woman scowled, clearly addressing a previous complaint from Frank.

"My boots are *m-i-s-s-i-n-g*." He called over his shoulder as he crossed back to his house.

The chief blew out a breath and rubbed a hand over her face. For a millisecond, her body softened. Then she straightened again. "We've been trying to call Alexandra. Her phone isn't working or in range, and she missed a meeting with me two days ago. That isn't like her. I *am* concerned. As far as the death of Viktor Walker, she is a person of interest but not a suspect currently. My detectives are handling this. But if we don't hear from her soon, we will have to issue an arrest warrant."

"I just want to know she is okay. I don't want to upset her life." Amanda whispered.

"Look." The chief took a step back. "I don't know what you expected or why you came here. You think you're trying to help. You say you're worried about Alexandra. Fine. But you must respect that she is an experienced investigator and knows what she is doing. And the job of finding out what happened here—that is for the police. You get in our way, and I will have you out of this town faster than you can shave a cat. I'm sticking to my 48-hour notice, now 40 hours, for you to find a new place to plant your van and business. You can leave a note for Alexandra and when she gets back, she can decide what to do with you."

Chief Rodriquez finished talking and turned to go.

Shave a cat? Amanda shuddered. As far as threats went, that was one of the scariest things she could think of and the strangest. But Amanda felt lucky she hadn't been arrested for meddling.

As Amanda picked up the laundry basket at her feet and headed towards the van, the chief called over her shoulder, "And be careful with that odd cat. For some reason, Alexandra is protective of him. Even though she has neighbors stopping in to put out food and water, you should consider taking it to a kennel if you are going to live in the house. It's got a finicky personality."

Amanda hurried across the lawn after the other woman. "Hey, it's not finicky or odd."

"You tell her." Grok wrapped around Amanda's legs, almost tripping her. Stepping towards the retreating police chief, the cat hissed and swung a paw at her back.

Fortunately, the other woman didn't notice and was soon in her police cruiser, driving slowly down the street.

"Well, that was—" Amanda didn't know what that was. But suddenly emboldened, she asked the cat, "Want more food while I finish the laundry?"

The cat gave her a very human grin.

Amanda left the basket of towels on the floor of the Pink Pup to be stowed away later, and she returned to the house with Grok.

TWENTY-TWO

The Jacket

When Amanda re-entered the house this time, she felt more comfortable. Somehow, in defending Grok, she had made herself at home. Sort of. It was still a mess, and there was no way she was sleeping here. But at least she could tidy it up, so Alexandra had a clean house to come home to.

Grok followed her into the kitchen and immediately rushed ahead to a cabinet in the kitchen. He pushed a paw along the door, like he had done it a hundred times before, and slid it open. Amanda had to wonder how many spaces were Grok-proofed in the house. Inside, Amanda found a bowl with Grok's name written on the side. "Is this what you're looking for?"

Grok trilled and gave her a smug look.

"Well, why didn't you tell me before?" Amanda placed the bowl on the counter and filled it with the rest of the bag of fresh cat food from the fridge.

Grok didn't answer, as his mouth was already full of food.

Amanda finished filling the bucket and scrubbed the counters and the floor while the cat ate. She nosed around while she worked.

The kitchen was stocked with basic items, nothing fancy: no InstaPot, Crock Pot, or baking pans. One bent baking sheet that may have been used—she picked at the substance—to melt plastic?

She opened the pantry door. Inside was an abundance of empty shelves. There was a bag of coffee, some salt and pepper, and a bag of sugar on one shelf. A fire extinguisher and a flat of Amanda's favorite instant noodles were on the other shelf. They had only come out a year ago.

What were the chances that her sister would have liked the same noodle brand as she did?

As she finished cleaning everything but the kitchen walls, Amanda wondered what else they might have in common after all this time. It cheered her and encouraged her to explore the rest of the house.

She wandered into the living room that Ben had boldly de-ghosted. It wasn't large. She noted the comfortable-looking chair and sofa in muted oranges and reds, its cushions all askew, pushed back against a coco-colored accent wall and built-in bookshelves, both with dust smudges on the sides.

A small round table sat between the furniture, and a longer, narrow rectangular table with more photographs sat by the front door.

Amanda studied the pictures she had previously just

glanced at. Behind their graduation photo were six more images, now lying flat on the surface. Lining the frames back up, Amanda noted that each contained her sister doing something Amanda had never considered: rock climbing, scuba diving, camping. Most of the photos had Chief Rodriguez in them next to her sister. One picture had the chief in a wedding gown holding hands with a short, smiling man in a tuxedo. Her sister was in that one, too, looking uncomfortable but smiling in a frothy dress.

Grok followed her around the house, seeming to encourage her investigation. Amanda could almost hear the cat's voice in her head telling her to find—something. What was she supposed to find?

She headed down the hallway.

Amanda used the kitchen towel over her shoulder at the first door, smearing the gray powder as she turned the handle and switched on the light. It was her sister's room. She stayed at the threshold. Tightly drawn blinds covered windows that ran along two sides. It was a decent-sized room, tidy. Alexandra hadn't left in a rush. Had she known she was going to be gone long?

Nothing inside had powder on it, and she wondered if the team could tell from the doorknob that the room hadn't been touched.

Amanda turned off the light and shut the door again. She might feel more comfortable in the house now, but she wasn't ready to invade her sister's privacy.

Three other doors led off the hallway. She opened one. It was a guest bathroom. Now, this room looked like it had been used recently. The forensic team must have thought so, too; dust covered the edges of most of the surfaces, and every drawer was half open with contents rifled through. The shower curtain was pushed back, and a used towel hung over the tub's edge. The hand towel was crumpled up on the floor. Why would the guest bathroom be messier than her sister's bedroom?

Amanda tried the other door in the hallway. It was locked. She pushed the third door. It led to a spacious guest bedroom. Flipping on the light, she could see the team spent a lot of time in this room. The comforter was crumpled like someone had been lying on top of it, and everything had been rifled through or moved.

Grok sped past her, sniffing every corner. When he got to the bed, he growled and jumped up on the pillow, poking his nose between the mattress and the headboard.

Amanda leaned in. "I don't see anything."

Grok hissed at her.

She tried again, kneeling and looking up from under the bed.

"Look deep." A voice commanded.

Amanda jerked back and looked up. Grok was on the bed staring at her like she was an idiot. He hissed and stuck his nose back into the tight space. Amanda shook it off and looked under the bed again. This time, she could see it. A dark cloth had slid down and was wedged between the mattress and the wall, not touching the floor. She reached for it, wiggling it loose until it fell to the floor. It was a jacket. Amanda pulled it out—a man's navy blue blazer.

What was that doing here? Did her sister have a boyfriend?

Amanda wrestled with her need to leave and her need to know and finally decided she should search the pockets. Reaching gingerly into the front pocket, she felt around. It was empty. She tried the other pocket and found a single key. She reached into the breast pocket, stabbing her finger into the corner of a hard piece of paper. She pulled it out. It was a business card.

Amanda read the name on the card aloud. "Viktor Walker, Owner, Walker Property Development."

Grok snarled from his perch on the pillow, tail swishing.

"It was no accident that he was found here. Viktor had been in this bedroom and undressed enough to leave his jacket. *Ewwww!* What else did he take off? Was he involved with my sister?" Amanda dropped the jacket. She studied the room.

She didn't know what she was looking for, and it had been a long day. She could use some food and an early night.

Picking the jacket back up, Amanda backed out of the room, shutting the door behind her, and retreated to the kitchen, where she draped the jacket over a kitchen chair and placed the key and the card in the middle of the table.

Amanda put on the kettle and studied the jacket while she waited for it to boil. She still had no answers as she poured hot water into her instant noodles and covered the top to let it soak. She refreshed Grok's water bowl and considered setting a place for herself at the kitchen table. It was a round pedestal table that looked mid-century and matched the rest of the furniture in the house.

She couldn't do it.

She grabbed the bowl of noodles and a spoon and retreated out to the Pink Pup, leaving the jacket behind.

Sitting in the van's passenger seat, she felt ridiculous for making such a big deal over the house. She could be sitting in there, much more comfortable. Or, she could have been eating with Ben if she hadn't been so stubborn. Or so afraid.

TWENTY-THREE

Voice Mail

While she ate her dinner, Amanda thought about the jacket on the chair in the kitchen. What should she do?

Through questioning the neighbors, she learned a lot of people didn't like Viktor Walker. But that didn't mean he was killed. He could have died of a heart attack. Well, not a heart attack. But maybe he had been sick? Sure, it was suspicious that it happened here in her sister's house. But perhaps her sister let Vik stay here. Maybe it was a coincidence that his wife was out of town, and the spare bedroom looked used, possibly by more than one person. But at least she was pretty confident her sister wasn't having an affair with Vik. Surely, she would have used her bedroom for that, and the jacket was found in the spare.

She had no idea what to think about the body being moved. But one thing was certain: she wouldn't be sleeping in that love nest tonight. She had a perfectly good air mattress in the Pink Pup.

Amanda worried that Grok didn't have any more food. Maybe her sister hadn't planned on being gone this long? The chief made it clear she was not to investigate her sister's disappearance. But a concern for Grok should be allowable. What if she asked the neighbors for help identifying who was feeding the cat and where she could get more food he liked? And if she happened to learn more about Viktor at the same time, well, that wasn't her fault.

As darkness settled outside the cab's window, Amanda finished her dinner and moved to the back of the van. She decided the jacket could wait until tomorrow.

She inflated her air mattress and pulled out her sister's casebook. But before opening the book, she took the paper out of her back pocket. The chief said Alexandra's phone wasn't working. But what if she was wrong?

Bracing herself, she turned on her phone. She had switched it off to avoid—things. As it powered up, a series of images flashed across the screen: the front of the house, the back, one of the living room. Then they vanished. She didn't remember taking photos of the house. She tried to find them again but got distracted by a little red dot indicating multiple missed calls and texts. She groaned. She couldn't keep doing this. She was going to have to deal with him sooner or later. Probably sooner, as she had to keep her phone on in case her sister or a client called.

She ignored the messages and punched in the numbers from the paper. She put it on speaker so she didn't drop it and accidentally disconnect. Heart racing, she waited for it to ring. But it didn't. It jumped straight to voicemail.

"Hello, you've reached Alexandra Warren. Please leave a message."

That was it. The starkness of the message fit with the Alexandra she knew from long ago—matter of fact and down to business.

Amanda burst into tears.

Grok wasn't sure what woke him. Moonlight streamed in through the window. He had been fed well and had the sofa to himself. What else did he need? He rolled over to go back to sleep when he heard a sound outside. A faint scratching on glass. Was that from the kitchen?

Grok flipped to his feet, crouched, and emitted a low rumbling warning growl. Hair bristled on his back as he arched.

Another scratch. Now, the noise came from right outside the front window.

Body tense, Grok swished his tail and waited.

Footsteps.

A shadow crossed the window, blocking the moonbeams that bathed the room in low light. A soft grunt. A curse. Were they trying to open the window? Were they trying to get in? Why?

Grok hissed, sinking into a hunting position and stilling as he swore an oath. "Not my house."

The shadow retreated.

A few seconds later, the front door handle turned, but it was locked.

Footsteps receded.

Grok jumped from the sofa and raced to the back of the house. He streaked through the dog door that Alexandra had installed. The door only opened to a chip she had inserted under his skin, one of many implants he wore, and it closed behind him. Grok disappeared into the darkness. He was hunting the prey that had come to him.

The Police

Amanda woke to the sound of an irate cat and a hangover—the kind you get from too much crying and not enough hydration. The casebook was stuck to her face, the elastic band leaving a deep groove.

She glanced at her phone, 6:34 in the "too early" morning. Grabbing a bottle of water, she stumbled to the door of the van.

Grok was sitting outside the door, making an unholy racket. An elongated howl tangled with a shriek like a coyote, terrifying and loud. When she opened the door, he added a chuffing sound and looked at Amanda with a hangry expression. Someone had a bad night.

"You are going to wake up the neighbors. What's wrong with you?"

He glared at her and made the chuffing sound again as if it was her fault she couldn't understand him. Was this what having a teenager was like?

Across the street, Frank came out of his house. He was

wearing a thick fleece and had a cup of coffee in his hands. He stopped when he heard the racket and pointed at Grok. "Everything okay?"

Amanda shivered. She was standing in the damp, foggy front yard in her pajamas. With the narrow street and almost no yards, Frank could probably see the bows and hats on the dogs in her puppy Christmas pajamas. She crossed her arm self-consciously over her chest. "Not sure. I think he is hungry."

"I'd feed him—fast," Frank said as he headed into his studio.

Amanda frowned at Grok. "Well, since you finished off all your food last night, I guess we will be going into town. Good thing Ben paid us yesterday, or you'd be getting instant noodles for breakfast."

Amanda had hoped for a shower this morning but instead crawled back into the van to pull on a clean pair of jeans and a T-shirt. As she yanked a sweatshirt over her head, she realized she needed to take Viktor's jacket with them and drop it off at the police station. She put on her raincoat and slid the casebook and a handful of business cards into the pocket. Stepping out of the van, she saw the fog had gotten thicker in just the few minutes she was inside.

"Hurry up." Someone growled from somewhere in the mist.

Amanda glanced around. "Hello?"

The fog parted. Grok was staring impatiently at her. Amanda shook her head. She needed coffee—lots of it.

"Hang on a second, I've got to grab the jacket." She

quickly unlocked the front door and went to the kitchen. As she folded up the jacket and put it in a plastic bag from under the sink, Amanda noted raindrops streaking the glass window of the back door. Good thing she had grabbed her raincoat. Relocking the front door, she glanced at the front window. It was also sprinkled with drops from the light rain the night before, and the grass was damp. And there, in the dirt under the window, was a fresh set of large footprints.

Most of the marks from the police had been washed away with the rain, so Amanda knew those hadn't been there last night and certainly not earlier in the day when she had walked the house's perimeter.

"Grok, look at that."

The cat turned up his nose and blew out a breath.

Amanda added the footprints to her list of things to report to the police this morning and followed Grok as he stalked down the street.

The eerie fog clouds started to lift on the walk into town. Amanda admired the houses with fancy trims and pastel colors lit by the pale morning light that made it through the mist. Some were huge and multi-story with gabled roofs, others tiny little studio-like homes on half lots, like Dot and Bert's. The yards were small or nonexistent—on many of them, she could have reached out and brushed the front door with her hand as she walked past. There were substantial mature oak and cypress trees and a surprising number of Redwoods. Even when she got to the main street, the town still had a park-like feel.

A big commercial building ran the entire block, the

front facade made to look like several different Victorian homes. There were retail shops on the ground floor and offices up above. The other side of the street looked similar, but it was broken up with a historic bank building that now housed an art gallery. Not many of the shops were open this early in the morning.

"Police first," Amanda said. Grok grumbled but followed her as she turned towards the station. It was only a couple of minutes walk from the downtown area.

This time, she entered through the front door and asked for Ben at the reception desk. A few minutes later, he emerged through a door into the lobby.

"What a surprise! What are you doing here so early?" Ben's smile was mixed with a puzzled frown. Under his windbreaker, a blue plaid shirt was buttoned to his chin.

"I wanted to get your opinion on a couple of things." Amanda felt self-conscious about seeking him out. Maybe she should have called the detective.

"What do you want to know?" Ben pulled her to the side of the lobby, his hand lingering on her arm.

Amanda had to dislodge the hand to pull the jacket out of the bag. "I found this in Alexandra's house. It's Viktor's. I wasn't sure what I should do with it."

Ben's face sobered. "Inside the house? Was that all you found?"

"Yes. The bed looked like someone had been lying on top of the comforter. But I didn't find anything else suspicious. Should I tell the police or return it to Sally?"

"Tell the police. I'll call Detective Kim right now, and he can join us."

Before Amanda could blink, Ben had his phone out and dialed a preset number. There was a brief conversation before Ben hung up. "He will be here soon. What else did you need?"

Amanda took a deep breath. She locked her fingers together and plunged ahead. "I wanted to, well, dinner. I'm sorry I didn't say yes yesterday. I should have. Do you want to try again? I mean, if you're free, that is, if you're not, I understand that's okay."

Ben stopped her. "I would love to come to dinner."

"Come to dinner? You mean me to cook? At Alexandra's?"

"No. I can bring takeout. You didn't stay in her house?"

"No. I slept in the van."

"Good. We will get it cleaned up so you'll be safe sleeping in the house. How about tonight? I'll bring the PPE and my Spray and Vac, and we will have a cleaning party."

"Okay." Amanda nodded as her mind raced. Had she just invited him to bring her food and clean her sister's house?

"What did you do now?" The sarcastic comment came from the end of the hall.

They turned to face Officer Hartman, sneering under his cheesy mustache. "Tick-tock, your time is running out. What did the chief say, 48 hours? Now it's down to 24 hours."

Detective Kim followed Officer Hartman through a

side door. Their soft-soled shoes made little squeaks on the linoleum as they approached.

"What's this I hear about a jacket?" The detective asked.

Amanda stretched out a hand to give him the jacket. "I found it between the mattress and the wall on the end of the guest bed. Well, Grok found it. I wasn't sure if you wanted it or if I should return it to Sally."

Detective Kim and Ben shared a concerned look. "Do you have gloves?" He asked Ben.

Ben pulled a pair from his pocket and passed them to the other man. After putting on the gloves, the detective reached for the jacket. He checked each pocket.

"Oh, I already searched the pockets. There's just a business card and a key."

All three men turned and looked at Amanda.

"Of course, you touched them." Officer Hartman made a sound of disgust.

"Why shouldn't I? What is going on?" Officer Hartman's comments made Amanda feel very stupid, and she didn't know why.

Ben grabbed her hand. "We are sure now that Viktor Walker didn't die of natural causes. He was murdered. I'm still waiting for the test results to find out how."

Amanda blinked, trying to process what Ben was saying. It was strange how thinking there might have been foul play and knowing he was murdered made everything so much more intense.

When Officer Hartman made another snorting sound,

the detective whipped around to face him. "That is enough."

The detective turned back to Amanda. "We will need to look at the scene again and ensure nothing else was missed."

"Well, you should know someone was outside the house last night. It rained, and there were footprints on the ground this morning."

The detective turned to the officer. "Head over there immediately. I'll log the jacket into evidence and meet you there." He turned back to Amanda. "Anything else?"

Wide-eyed, Amanda shook her head.

The detective left with the jacket.

"We might have to push that dinner to tomorrow night," Ben said with a pat on her arm.

TWENTY-FIVE

Breakfast

Shoulders slumped, mind wandering, Amanda was back at the Monarch Deli & Café several blocks from the police station, staring at a menu. When the waitress returned, she realized she hadn't been looking at it, so she handed it back and asked for a double order of scrambled eggs and a black coffee.

"And bacon." Said a voice from the next table.

"And bacon," Amanda added. The waitress left before Amanda could take it back.

She turned around to give the man behind her an annoyed look, but there was no one there.

Grok wove around her legs and jumped up on the chair beside her.

"Oh no. You are sitting on the floor to eat." She informed him, pushing him off the chair.

He was the one giving her the annoyed look now. But when the waitress returned with a saucer of cream for him and their order, he settled in next to a potted plant to eat breakfast.

Amanda couldn't believe the police were at the house again. She should have never snooped around. One thing was for sure: she wasn't going back into that house. She was done with dead bodies. And sticky black powder that got on everything. And icky dead body cooties. But then, there was her sister. Missing. Somewhere out there on her own and Amanda not with her. Again.

No. She wasn't going to leave her sister hanging again. There must be something she could do to help. Maybe the spiral-bound notebook had a clue.

She pulled the book from her pocket. It had a plain black cover and an elastic strap that secured it shut. She added milk and sugar to her coffee and then spread the book on the table beside her. The notes were neatly organized and broken into sections; each seemed dedicated to a different client. The names weren't listed. But there was a case number at the top of each section. Most of it was a logbook with dates, times, and initials. Maybe they signified locations and people?

She quickly searched on her phone. MRY could mean Monterey, CML for Carmel, SEA for Seaside. If she was right, there were other locations, too, but most were in California.

The other initials were more challenging to decipher. There were four sections, and a different set of initials dominated each, so Amanda decided they were either a client or a suspect: RS, BN, FM, and RMC. Who could they be? None of the cases looked closed out. The way

Amanda read it, there were four main clients her sister was working for when she disappeared.

Amanda flipped to the end of each section. The first case had an entry ten days ago. The next two had dates from six and seven days ago. The last one had a date from three days ago and read, "RMC drove 2 Last Chance ML and met with BR."

Amanda's heart raced. Three days ago!

It had been at least two days since anyone saw Alexandra. After her last entry, she must have returned to the house and left the journal. But where did she go after that? Was she at the house when Viktor was killed?

If she showed this to Chief Rodriquez, would it help clear her sister as a suspect? Or make it worse? And what if the chief thought she was interfering and took the journal?

And it didn't mean that RMC, or any of the people in the journal, had anything to do with her sister disappearing or Viktor's death.

Amanda wasn't sure what to do next. She sighed, pushing aside the last of her breakfast and laying her head on folded arms on the table. She was so tired. Why did Grok have to wake her up so early?

Her phone rang next to her ear. Startled, she bolted up and almost answered it, but then she saw the number and pushed the call to voicemail. Immediately, the phone started to ring again. As she automatically repeated the gesture, she suddenly stopped when she saw the number and answered instead. "Hello?"

"This is Detective Kim of the Ocean Wood Police

Department. We've found a series of footprints around the house, and the window on the backdoor was broken."

Amanda thought of the rain she had seen streaking the window that morning. "It wasn't like that when I left!"

"We think we disturbed whoever was trying to enter the house. We will have a cruiser in this area for the rest of the day. We wanted to let you know so you could stay alert and be aware that you should board up the window. We will be leaving soon."

Amanda thanked the officer for the call and hung up. What a mess. She might not know where Alexandra was, but she could stay and try to clear her name and protect her house. And that meant she needed income so even if she moved to a new location, she could stay close by.

She paid the bill and then asked the waitress if she could leave some of her business cards. The waitress pointed to a bulletin board by the bathroom. Amanda pinned several cards there and then, pulling another handful from her pocket, headed out to the wakening town of Ocean Wood.

Deliciously satisfied, Grok was content to follow Amanda around as she ran her errands. After all, she had fed him. Besides, if the police were still at the house, he didn't want to see them rifling through his things again.

The sun came out, and warmth spread along the fur of

his back, making his muscles loose. He had to shorten his strides to follow Amanda's hesitant steps as she twisted left and right, fretting. This one was constantly worrying over something. What a waste of time. A predator attacked, you dealt with it, you didn't worry about it. If he was inclined, he could teach her. She seemed malleable and could be very useful to him.

He considered this as she finally picked a path and took off across the street. The relaxed glow of his full belly did not last long. No sooner had they stepped onto the road when he spotted the long white vehicle of the veterinarian clinic.

He skidded to a stop as his body shuddered. He couldn't retreat. He would be seen. Escape route options raced through his mind and on instinct, he took the first one. As he turned down the side alley by the travel agency, he ran for the back to get out of view of the vehicle.

The veterinary clinic was his least favorite place on Earth. Alexandra had taken him there when she first found him wandering alone in the forest. He was wounded and confused, and before he could stop them, they had doped him up and, without permission, stuck probes in every hole.

What were they looking for? Oh yes, consent! And they didn't have it from him.

He had never gone back.

But recently, he started having dizzy spells and blacking out whenever he tried to remember his past. Alexandra had talked to him about making an appointment.

He took a hard pass on that idea.

He could understand everyone around him, no matter the language they spoke. But he had no idea how she was planning to explain to the vet that she could understand him when he talked, and that was how she knew he was having memory issues. They would think she was a nutter. Maybe she was.

Grok jumped up on the lid of a green dumpster, then on top of an RV parked behind the building, and up to a second-story balcony.

Ducking, he entered through the window. Someone shrieked.

He quickly raced out of the room into the hall. He had been in this building before and knew they kept the attic stairs unlocked. He knew a lot about the things happening in this town that the people living here had no clue were going on.

What he didn't know was why Alexandra and he had this psychic connection. He didn't have it with anyone else. He knew it wasn't normal for animals and humans on this planet. But that was the thing. Even not knowing *who* he was, he knew he didn't fit here. He was something more than the animals around him. His higher reasoning and self-awareness was evolved beyond even that of the humans here.

He emerged on the roof and padded on four paws to the edge, looking down on the parking below. And he was smart enough to know to avoid that white vehicle and the tall man that drove it.

A seagull called out as it flew past. Grok followed its

path with a pang of longing. He loved flying. A memory surfaced: a flash of joy surging through his body as he flew through a blood-red sky.

A stabbing pain shot through his head, and he weaved on the edge of the roof. He had a brief awareness of muscle weakness before his limbs collapsed, and he dug in his claws to keep from rolling off the side of the building as the memory disappeared and left a piercing agony.

He panted, vision spotty, and tried to regain his strength. Alexandra usually cared for him when he had one of these spells—dragging his huge body back to the house and microwaving something tasty for him. She was a terrible cook. He missed her. Talking with her kept the loneliness at bay. Her obsession with understanding him was annoying, but she fed him regularly and was teaching him Earth games and how to read the primitive scratches they called writing in this place. So, not too much to complain about. Except that now she was gone, and he couldn't remember why.

As he rolled onto his back, squirming in the gravel that covered the roof, he considered the sister. Amanda had surprised him. He was starting to think there was more to her than met the eye. She responded to his questions almost as if she understood him.

Could he talk with her psychically, too?

He had been running a series of experiments to test her intellect and ability. Moving things and seeing if she missed them. Saying phrases and seeing if she would repeat them. She didn't seem aware yet that he was doing it. But once he was convinced his little study was a success, he planned on having a face-to-face discussion with her—if that didn't scare her off, then this could be another promising relationship.

Feeling better, he pushed to his feet and looked over the ledge. The white vehicle was parked almost directly beneath him, and the tall man was getting out.

Grok must have been spotted. He prepared himself to run.

But the tall man walked away, crossing the street and heading in the direction Amanda had gone.

Grok considered warning her, but the man had never done anything to Alexandra. He assured himself that he wasn't running like a coward. No, he was returning to the house to monitor the police's investigation, far from the probing tools of the vet.

TWENTY-SIX

New Business

Amanda's nerves were jumping under her skin at the prospect of having to sell her services. Having Grok here was grounding. It made her feel like she was part of a team again. She liked it.

Crossing the street, she entered the first shop open, holding the door for Grok, but the cat had disappeared.

Amanda stepped back out and looked up, then down the street. No sign of Grok. Her shoulders slumped. Taking a breath, she stepped back into the store and peered around old oak cabinets and cherry wood tables, looking for someone, anyone. No one was inside.

"Hello?" she called out and waited. No answer.

Her shoulders slumped.

Exiting, she went into the next open shop. This store had racks of linen women's clothing and gold and silver jewelry hanging in the window.

"Good morning?" Amanda's greeting came out more

like a question. She tried to smile and look friendly as she leaned in the door.

"Good morning, come in." A smartly dressed woman was rearranging a stand of women's hats while she talked to an older man wearing a subdued Hawaiian shirt. "Let me know if I can help you find anything." The woman smiled.

Amanda disliked this part of her business but smiled and took a deep breath. "I was wondering if I could leave you some business cards. I'm new in town and trying to get local clients for my mobile dog grooming business." The words gushed out. Amanda blushed. "Sorry, I can repeat that."

The man laughed and reached out a hand for a card. "No, we got it. Mobile dog grooming. Did you try the Best Friend Boutique? I bet they'd love to know an alternative groomer is in town."

"I didn't. Where is that?" Amanda's face lit up with a genuine smile.

"Next block. Give me a couple of cards, and I'll put them next door in my shop. My name's Herb. Do I know you? You look familiar." The man studied her face.

She hadn't considered how many people would recognize her face in town. "My twin sister lives here. I'm visiting. My name's Amanda."

"And I'm Linda. Twins? Really? You two must look stunning when you are together. I'll add a couple of cards to our board." Gold bracelets chimed as the woman brushed a strand of perfectly styled platinum hair out of her eyes and reached for the cards.

Amanda handed a stack to each and thanked them before leaving.

"That was a good start." She said to herself as she carried on down the street.

The next shop was closed, and the one after that was a bakery. She decided to leave it for last. The next few shop owners politely took a few cards. She kept passing people walking their dogs and took the presence of dog owners as a good sign.

Amanda looked left as she crossed the street and stopped, stunned. The road dipped down, and she had a fantastic view out over the tops of the houses to the ocean in the Monterey Bay. The vivid blue water called to her.

"I'll see you as soon as I get some work going." She told the ocean under her breath and forced herself to keep moving.

The next block had individual buildings pushed so close together that a piece of paper couldn't have slid between them. Painters in white pants and shirts were climbing ladders in front of the first shop, so she skipped it and went to the next one. A metal water bowl was outside the store, and across the sidewalk, patio seating had been set up. Too late for breakfast, too early for lunch, the tables were all empty, and the restaurant was locked. Amanda pushed on. The next shop had a big red heart on the door and a fancy script reading "Best Friend Boutique."

Amanda admired the raised double water bowl to the side and the "pets welcome" sign in the window. A bell rang as she entered the shop.

"We are closing soon for lunch." A monotone voice called from somewhere in the shop.

Amanda glanced at her phone. It wasn't even 10 AM yet. "I wanted to talk to the owner. Are they here?" Her voice pitched up at the end.

A young woman with a low-cut blouse and tight jeans stalked out of a back room. "What do you want with the owner?"

"I'm a dog groomer, and I was hoping to leave some of my cards here in case any of your customer's pets needed grooming."

Amanda handed over a card. The woman flipped a wave of silky blond hair over her shoulder and took the card. Holding it on the tips of inch-long nails, she scowled as she studied the paper like it was a parking ticket, then she handed it back to Amanda. "We have a preferred groomer. We don't need another one."

Amanda was stunned as the young woman turned and left the room, leaving Amanda alone in the shop. Not sure what to do, she left.

The rest of the shop owners were far more receptive; several took cards and listened to her spiel about services. She crossed back over the street and canvased the shops on the other side.

Amanda stopped at a travel agency and looked in the window. The faded display was of a teddy bear posed with luggage in front of sun-bleached photos of tropical locations and World Heritage sites. Maybe someday. Amanda cupped her hand over the glass and peered in. The agency was closed. All the lights and computers were off. Shame.

The travel agency's building was on a corner, and she looked both ways as she crossed the street. On her left, in the parking lot behind the travel agency, she saw the nervous neighbor, Anh Nguyen, climbing into a huge Class A motorhome. She thought about going over to say "hello" but remembered how unfriendly he had been and continued with her task.

"Alexandra!" Someone called behind her. The sound of feet pounding on the pavement and the name was said several times. Amanda realized they were talking to her. She felt a hand on her arm. "Alexandra!"

She whirled around and looked up and up into the attractive face of a man in his late 30s. He put his hands on his knees, panting to catch his breath. That put him at face level with her. "Hello?"

"Why didn't you stop? I saw you earlier, and I've been trying to catch you. Why did you miss your appointment? You made such a big deal about needing an emergency visit, then you didn't show."

Amanda didn't know what to say.

"I've been slammed these last few days. Everyone has a sick animal. I'm just coming back from a house call, and there you were. What is going on?" The man stood up to his full height again.

He knew something!

Amanda's heart raced as she leaned back and looked up at him. "When was Alexandra's appointment?"

Scrunching his eyebrows together, the man glared down at her. "You're going to pretend you didn't wake me up at dawn three days ago and demand an appointment for a CT scan and blood work for Grok, then not show up? I suppose you are going to pretend we don't have a date this weekend, too? What is going on?"

"I'm not Alexandra!" Amanda blurted out as soon as the man stopped talking. She shook her head when he glared at her. "I'm not. I'm her twin sister Amanda. Alexandra has disappeared. Did she tell you where she was going? Why was she bringing Grok to you—did she say what was wrong with him?"

The man leaned down uncomfortably close and, with narrowed eyes, studied her face. "I'm—I —I don't know what to say. It's incredible. You aren't Alexandra, are you?" He only paused for a minute before adding. "Where is she?"

Amanda shook her head. "I don't know. She disappeared. The police are looking for her, too." Amanda didn't go into the details of why. "What did she tell you?"

As if suddenly aware that he was in her face, the man stood up and stepped back. "She said Grok was having memory issues. Said it was urgent we test him. She told me she had to check something out and then would bring him in for the scans and tests. She was precise on what type, so I thought he had been in an accident. A CT scan would tell us if there were any fractures or bleeding. Then she wanted a blood test for parasites and DNA tests, a whole genome sequencing. I thought it was a bit overboard and wouldn't help me treat an injury, but she insisted."

"I have to call the detective." Amanda's hand shook as

she pulled out her phone. While waiting for the call to connect, she studied the tall man before her, then said, "You may have been the last person to talk to her before she disappeared."

TWENTY-SEVEN

Casebook

The detective wasn't there, so Amanda left a message with the vet's name, Dr. Val Klimmer. Afterward, the doctor apologized again for the misidentification and left.

Amanda started walking back to the house. Maybe Grok should have scheduled an appointment. She felt terrible that she had been concerned about how to pay for his high-end meals while he could have been bleeding internally. She wished he was with her so the doctor could have looked him over.

However, having worked out of a veterinarian's office her entire career, she had seen a lot of sick animals; besides being cranky, impatient, and demanding, nothing had alerted her to a more significant issue with the cat.

Her phone rang. She almost answered it without looking but remembered to check the numbers at the last minute. It was Detective Kim.

"Hello."

"Amanda, I heard you left me a message?"

Amanda repeated what she had learned to the detective and passed on the vet's name and number. "Surely, this means Alexandra wasn't in town before the murder. Have you still not been able to locate her?"

The detective sighed. "No. We don't know where she is. I can't comment on an active investigation. But this doesn't clear her or indicate it was her in any way. We will keep looking for her."

Amanda leaned against the brick wall beside her, hiding in the shadow of the building. The day was beautiful, and she wasn't in any frame of mind to enjoy it.

"We are almost done here. You can come back to the house anytime."

Amanda said goodbye and hung up, then muttered, "Until the chief kicks me out."

It was nearly lunchtime. Mentally counting the money left in her pocket, she headed for a grocery she had seen further down the street.

Passing a realty office on the way, she glanced at the framed home listings hanging in the window. The top row of homes was gorgeous—multi-level modern designs with spacious backyard pools and ocean views. The numbers listed under them made her choke.

That couldn't be the price!

The next row of houses was more modest, like the ones she had passed on the way into town; a lot of Victorians, some Craftsman-style, and several stucco-covered. They were small, two and three-bedroom homes, but their prices—Amanda's eyes bulged.

Were they kidding?

How had Alexandra afforded to live in this town? Maybe cops got paid a lot more here?

Amanda didn't know what police salaries were in Ohio. She knew what her ex paid his staff because she did the books. Working for her husband from college until she'd left him, she had never pulled a salary. Everything went back into the business. She felt like a fool.

Melancholy swept over her, and a second later, something brushed her knee. She looked down. Grok was winding through her legs, purring. "Where have you been?" She tried to sound chiding, but she was so happy to see him that she risked reaching down and giving the cat a thank-you pat on the head before she continued walking.

A wooden sign over the door said, "Cypress Market." The low white building was domed like a Quonset hut and stretched the entire width of a town block. The inside was more extensive than it looked outside.

Amanda found bread, the cheapest, sliced cheese on sale, then splurged on a jar of bread and butter pickles and a head of prewashed lettuce. She also got milk for coffee. After she made her purchases, she found several tables to the side of the checkout counter and settled at one to make a sandwich.

Pulling out Alexandra's journal, Amanda laid it on the table beside her to read while she ate. "It just doesn't make any sense to me. How would I even know if one of these cases was about Viktor?" She muttered as she flipped quickly through several coded pages.

The cat was staring. Amanda felt judged. "I'm trying

to figure it out, but I'm not an investigator like Alexandra." She defended herself.

The cat cocked a brow, or maybe it was a head tilt, but she got the idea. Okay. Perhaps she should have told the police about the notebook. But her sister wasn't under arrest yet, so she had convinced herself the casebook wouldn't interest anyone else.

Amanda flipped back to that last entry again. If three days ago was the last time her sister was at the house, it couldn't have been her that killed Viktor. "How was he killed?" she muttered.

She heard the word "Poison."

Amanda looked up and Grok glared at her. That was odd. Had she said that out loud? She guessed he could have been poisoned. But would that have happened at Alexandra's house? How long did it take poison to work?

She could only focus on one mystery at a time and flipped pages to the beginning of the last section, with the most recently dated entry, and tried reading through the personal observations. It was no use. She didn't understand the code. But there was something familiar about it that tickled a long-forgotten memory.

Why did Alexandra always have to be so cryptic? Even when they were kids, Alexandra was always the cerebral one. While Amanda wanted everyone to be happy, Alexandra wanted to figure things out.

She spotted the initials VW. A few sentences later, they were followed by SW. Could that be Viktor and Sally Walker? A few sentences further, there was a list of ten more initials. One of them was CC. Could that be the neighbor Colleen Cooper? But what did the rest of it say? She might have the key to some hidden neighborhood secret that had gotten Vik killed and possibly threatened her sister, and she couldn't read it.

Frustrated, she flipped the journal closed and sat back in a huff.

"Excuse me, does your shirt say, 'Pink Power Wash and Groom?' Is that you?" A voice asked.

Amanda looked down at the words on the pink shirt she wore. She had forgotten she had it on. She turned towards the voice. "I am. Would you like a business card?" She rummaged around in her bag for more cards.

"I have one, thank you. I was hoping to book a visit for my dog. Would you have time this afternoon?"

Amanda pushed back in her seat. Her arms flailed as two legs of the chair left the ground, and she was airborne for a second. She all but shouted at the woman when she regained her footing and could stand to face her. "Yes!"

The tall, striking brunette suppressed a laugh. She wore a long-sleeve blue shirt, a silver puffer vest, and comfortable-looking jeans that hugged her ample curves. "Great, here is my address."

Amanda deflated. "I'm not quite mobile yet. I'm sorry."

"But you plan to be?" The woman asked.

"Yes, as soon as I get some gas."

"Well, this time, I can come to you. Where do you live?"

Amanda rattled off the address. The woman frowned. "Isn't that Alexandra's house?"

"You know my sister?" Amanda wasn't sure why she was surprised. "I am staying there while she's gone. But my mobile grooming van will be mobile again soon, and then I'll be available for any location."

"That's why you look so familiar. Well, I am happy to give you a try. How about in a half hour?"

Amanda nodded in agreement, and the woman left.

She had a client.

Amanda did a super quick happy dance and raced out of the store. Then she stopped and ran back in. She swept her bag of groceries and the case book off the table and called to Grok, "Come on!"

A grumpy Grok followed her out of the shop.

TWENTY-EIGHT

Restock

Amanda practically ran the rest of the way back to the house.

She arrived at her sister's house just as the police were locking up.

"Can I go in?" She asked the officer who was leaving. He pointed back to the next officer in line, who pointed to Officer Hartman, who gave another of his famous snorts and pointed to Detective Kim.

"Yes, you can go in. You are clear to use the house again." The detective confirmed. "But we are holding on to the key from the jacket as evidence. Do you have your own?"

"One of the neighbors gave me their key."

The detective's lips thinned. "And who was that?"

Amanda explained where she had gotten the key and which neighbors were supposed to have one.

"Interesting. Thank you for sharing this information. I may need you to come to the station and sign a statement."

"Fine, fine, can I do that tomorrow?" Amanda was starting to worry that her client would arrive soon and be put off by all the police.

At that moment, a silver SUV pulled up. The brunette got out and opened the back door. A young Golden Retriever jumped out and danced around the woman's legs.

Amanda bounced up on her toes. She loved Goldens; they had the most beautiful energy.

The brunette surveyed the scene and, instead of being put off, seemed thrilled at the drama. She made a beeline for the detective.

Amanda realized she didn't know her client's name.

"Detective." The woman purred when she arrived, giving the officer a sultry look.

"Katrina."

Amanda watched as the Asian man in his forties blushed like a teenage boy. It started at his neck and went to his ears.

"I'll just run in and put away the groceries while you catch up." Amanda left the detective at Katrina's mercy.

She entered the house and wondered where Grok was. He had left her on her way back from the market, and she hadn't seen the cat since. She wasn't too worried. She doubted the cat would get lost in the town.

She glanced at the living room as she passed through. Nothing seemed different. Still a mess. Still covered in fingerprint dust. Perhaps the police hadn't found anything new.

Amanda entered the kitchen. Glass littered the ground

around the back door, and a large hole punched in the window. After her appointment, she would have to look in the shed to see if Alexandra had anything that would cover it up.

She put her grocery bag on the counter, opened the fridge, and froze. The fridge's top shelf was packed with at least a dozen new cat food packages.

How had that gotten in there? Was her sister back? Had the person broken in to stock the fridge? No, that was too weird to even consider.

She looked around the kitchen for anything else different or out of place. Except for the broken window, it all looked the same. The spoon she had used last night was still in the dish rack. The towel was crumpled in the same place she had left it on the counter.

Why did something strange happen every time she came into this house?

TWENTY-NINE

Puddy

As her client was flirting with Detective Kim, Amanda tidied up the van, hiding her sleeping mat and bag. Then she set up for the appointment, putting out her favorite shampoos for goldens and the other tool she would need to make the dog look its best. Slapping the magnet on the door with her new phone number, she waited for Katrina to finish her conversation.

The detective looked relieved to see her. "Amanda, a minute of your time." The detective drew her off to the side of the house. He pointed to the ground.

Boot prints ran along the side of the house like the ones she had found outside the window this morning.

"They are all around the house and by the broken window. We've taken photographs. We don't know if it's related to the murder, but I'll have a police patrol car coming by a couple of times a night to check out the neighborhood. Be extra careful the next few days."

Amanda watched as the detective went out to his car and left.

As soon as the detective was out of sight, Grok appeared.

The retriever and the cat sniffed and then proceeded to ignore each other.

"How did you meet the mighty fine Detective Kim?" The brunette leaned in, eager for gossip.

"Unfortunately, I met him at the scene of a crime."

At the woman's raised brow, Amanda volunteered a quick summary of the events, including the news about Viktor's death.

"Couldn't have happened to a nastier guy. Viktor was a snake and the worst landlord."

At Amanda's startled look, Katrina's mouth twisted, and she added, "He owned the lease on our shop and was always raising the rent or accusing us of not taking care of the trash properly. I showed him proof that it wasn't us, but he'd never admit he was wrong."

"That's terrible, but a snake?" Amanda probed for a bit more information.

"He's been rumored to pressure women into sleeping with him. Nothing violent, but I would guess a little black-mail wouldn't be out of character. And then he would brag about it. It must be awful to live with. But I suspect his wife knew and looked the other way."

Amanda mulled over the new information. It told her more about Viktor's character. She was glad to have never met him in life. But it didn't tell her why he was in Alexandra's house. She really hoped they weren't having an affair.

Would she have made a date with the vet if she was also sleeping with Vik?

Amanda felt a wet tongue on her hand. She held her hand out for the Golden to sniff. "And who do we have here?"

"This is Buddy. He's a doll but impossible to keep clean. His sister, Bonny, is a show dog, but Buddy's got the wrong energy for it. If you do well with him, we might give you a chance to groom Bonny." The brunette raised her eyebrow in a challenge.

"I would be thrilled. I have groomed show dogs before, but it's been a few years."

She turned her attention back to Buddy. After he accepted her, Amanda chucked him under the chin, and the young golden sat back on his haunches and closed his eyes, leaning into her hand.

"I'm Katrina, by the way. I'd love to hear all about your experience. Can we chat while you work?"

Amanda hesitated, "You know it's going to get hairy in there."

Katrina laughed. "Oh, I know."

Amanda agreed and led them into the Pink Pup. Having someone to talk to other than her pet client was a treat. While Amanda gave Buddy a pre-bath brush, Katrina asked about her experience grooming. Amanda explained her background of working closely with a veterinarian and told the woman about her show dog experience. Katrina seemed impressed, and they talked back and forth while she worked.

Before Amanda knew it, she bathed and toweled

Buddy and moved him to the grooming table. She handed Katrina ear protection and pulled a head wrap over Buddy's ears so she could blow him dry.

Grok, who had curled up on a table in the corner, decided to leave for this part of the service.

Amanda heard a clear demand as the cat jumped off the counter and passed her. "Check his paw."

Surprised, she looked at Katrina, but the woman was still trying to put on the headphones so they wouldn't mess up her hair.

Just to be safe, Amanda rechecked each of the dog's paws. The front ones were clear, but in the back right paw, Buddy had a foxtail that was just starting to burrow its way in.

Amanda grabbed her tweezers and pulled the barb out. Buddy gave her hand a lick in appreciation.

That had to have been Katrina's voice, right? There is no way that Grok told her to check the dog's paws. But the woman was wearing ear protection and was engrossed in her phone.

Shaking her head, Amanda went back to drying the dog.

Buddy, for the most part, seemed to be enjoying his spa time. He loved to have his back scratched, his ear scratched, and his belly scratched. Scritching was Buddy's' favorite thing.

When he was dry, Amanda and Katrina removed her ear protection.

"What kind of cut would you like?" Amanda threaded her fingers through Buddy's coat.

"What do you suggest?" Katrina asked.

Amanda thought about it and had to admit, "I don't like to over-groom goldens. I usually use blending shears to clean up their legs, ears, and tails and spend most of my time finishing their undercoat. That way, he can show off his good features, and he'll be a little less work for you. Bonny would get a different cut since she shows."

Katrina nodded her head. "I like it. Why don't you tell me more about what brought you here and how long you plan to stay?"

Amanda thought about that question as she picked up her scissors to trim. "Honestly, I don't know how long I'm staying. I had hoped to figure that out after meeting my sister, but she's not here."

Amanda was glad to have the dog to focus her attention on. Talking about her plans made her uncomfortable. Everything she thought she wanted from life hadn't turned out as expected. Seeing her sister's life so different from hers left her wondering about all her mistakes. She had a second chance now, but what if she made a wrong decision and screwed it up?

She wrapped up Buddy's treatment and gently helped him off the table. Katrina pulled open the door, and Buddy bounded out of the vehicle and gave himself a massive shake. Amanda followed them out. "Well, what do you think?"

"I think I have a new groomer." Katrina grinned as she crouched down and hugged Buddy, burying her face in his coat and breathing deeply.

Amanda laughed, "I do that all the time. Nothing smells as yummy as a freshly cleaned dog."

"I knew I liked you. I'd like to bring his sister by tomorrow. Do you have time?"

"Of course."

Katrina pulled out her wallet. After paying, she shook her head and smiled. "I haven't been completely honest with you. I own a shop in town, 'Best Friend Boutique, a luxury pet destination.'" She spread her hands wide as she recited the tagline.

Amanda laughed at the theatrics.

"We have a groomer we recommend, but she's not very —good. I'm not sure she likes animals at all. I've been looking for a replacement. I would love to be able to refer clients to you for however long you are in town. Would that be okay?"

Amanda couldn't believe her luck and quickly agreed, thanking her.

"You deserve it. Buddy looks great."

Amanda remembered the bag in her purse. "Can I ask you a question before you go?"

At the woman's nod, Amanda grabbed her purse from the nook she had stashed it in and pulled out the cat food bag. "Are you familiar with this?"

Katrina whistled, "That is a very expensive brand. Super healthy, all-natural, and fresh, with no additives. Is it for Grok?"

"You know Grok?" Amanda was surprised.

"He's infamous. He has all the dogs and cats tied in knots when he is around, and some of the people, too.

Somehow, he knows all the hidden passages in town. You'll find him pop up everywhere." She nodded at the package, "It will cost a lot, but I can order it online for you or show you where to buy it, and they will deliver it right to you."

"Not yet, but I'll keep that in mind." Amanda tucked the bag back into her purse.

"Whenever you are ready. And I'll see you tomorrow for Bonny." As Katrina and Buddy left, they walked the short drive like a catwalk.

Amanda cleaned the Pink Pup and wondered about her sister's relationship with her neighbors, particularly with Viktor. She had only seen him dead, which wasn't a great time to judge a person's attractiveness. But he was quite a bit older than her. Honestly, age didn't bother her. She was more concerned with the womanizing several people had mentioned. She couldn't imagine her sister in a relationship like that.

She needed to learn more. How could she talk to the neighbors again without tipping off the chief or the detective that she was asking questions?

THIRTY

The Ocean

When Amanda finished cleaning the van after Buddy's appointment, she realized she had nothing more on her agenda for the day. She had postponed her dinner with Ben because she thought the police would still be at the house, but they were gone. With her cleaning wrapped up, she had at least three hours until sunset.

She searched her suitcase for a jacket pulling out a bright magenta zippered hoody with little white bones that read "Pink Power Wash & Groom" on the back and put it on along with her sister's knit cap in swirls of pink and green. Then she locked up the van.

"Grok, I'm going to the beach. Want to come?"

Lounging on the loveseat on the front porch, the cat ignored her.

Amanda's sneakers crunched on the gravel as she hurried across the drive.

Late afternoon was a quiet time on Lilly Street. None

of the neighbors were out; she could study their houses without feeling like she was snooping.

Frank's studio garage door was closed. The large SUV Frank drove and his husband's Mercedes were missing from the front of their house. She wondered what had happened between Frank and Vik. The level of animosity Frank still held towards Vik told her he hadn't gotten over it. He had a real motive for murder.

Amanda snorted out an exclamation in disbelief. Murder?

She took in a shuddering breath as she thought about the last few months living with her ex-husband. He had stolen years of her life and used her for free labor to build his business. Then, the cheat had given it all to his mistress. Amanda had been working so hard to keep both businesses afloat that she never saw the signs.

Or maybe she just stopped looking.

But she didn't hate him. She had exhausted all the emotions she had to spend on him long ago. Now she just wanted to move on, restart her life someplace new.

Ocean Wood could be that place. If only she knew how her sister felt about her. That betrayal hurt the most, maybe because she was the betrayer. She had made so many bad decisions in her life. Was staying here another one?

The excitement she'd started her walk with had drained away by the time she turned right onto Cypress Avenue.

A burst of salty ocean air drifted by on the wind,

teasing her nose and stirring her interest. She kept walking, following the scent.

Passing Driftwood Drive, she looked down the street and saw the teal and grey peak of the Walkers' Victorian towering over the rest of the block. Poor Sally to lose her husband that way. She wouldn't wish that fate on anyone.

After several blocks, the road took a gentle turn. Both sides of the tree-lined street had hotels and motels, all named with a variation of Cypress or Monarch, for the butterfly sanctuary that was somewhere around here. The gently sloping road ended at a T into Asilomar Avenue. Across the street was a fenced-in lighthouse surrounded by a golf course.

Amanda remembered Ben had taken a left when they went to the conference grounds. Now, she turned right and immediately glimpsed the ocean at the end of the road.

The lighthouse on her left, she picked up the pace as the water called to her. The sidewalk continually disappeared and reappeared on opposite sides of the street. As she negotiated the parked cars, she kept her attention on the light traffic, ensuring she didn't step out in front of a moving vehicle.

Distracted, she was completely unprepared when she looked up and saw the steel blue-gray of the Pacific Ocean beyond the grassy slopes of the golf course.

She passed several Cyprus trees and crossed the street to enjoy the sweeping view. White waves crashed on the rocky shore, sprays leaping several feet into the ominous gray sky. Amanda wondered if she should have brought a raincoat.

Her phone rang, she glanced at the screen, then pressed ignore on the number. A series of images from around Alexandra's house flashed on the screen. Why was that happening? The photos disappeared before she could figure out where they came from, and she shoved her phone into her pocket, determined to ignore it.

A brisk wind whipped in from the ocean. It was much colder than she had expected. She zipped her jacket to her chin, making a note to update her wardrobe as soon as possible.

A seagull called out, and Amanda looked up, tracing its white form against the sky.

She debated which way to go and randomly turned right towards the bay.

A winding trail made of fine gravel followed the shore. A dog walker or couple would pass every hundred yards, most with wind jackets and hats. They gave friendly nods and kept moving, which suited her perfectly.

A calm had settled over her since she had taken her first lungful of the crisp, salty air. The rumbling in her head stilled, and for the first time in months, maybe years, she found herself just being. It was the kind of peace she usually only felt when grooming. It made her lean towards the water, yearning for more.

Amanda didn't know how long she was on the trail before she heard the first deep, throaty bark. She could tell a lot of dog breeds from their bark, but she had never heard anything like this before.

Glancing around, she caught movement past the shore and watched as a dark sea lion emerged from the water and tried to heave itself onto a protected rock already occupied. The larger sea lion protested and head-butted the intruder. A couple stopped beside her, and they all watched the show.

"Big bully." The man next to her noted. He was in his late sixties and had a vented sun hat looped under his chin to keep it from flying off.

"No, he's just protecting his rock." The woman with him protested the many layers of her scarf flapping in the breeze behind her.

They watched as the animals pushed and shoved at each other until a third sea lion, bigger than the others, saw a chance and smoothly slipped between the battling animals, pushing them both into the cold water and taking the perch for themselves.

The show concluded, and Amanda continued walking.

The sun came out; the grey sky was quickly replaced by a vivid blue with wispy clouds. Feeling hot in her hoodie, Amanda unzipped the front half-way and pushed up the sleeves.

Pulling out her phone, she called up a map. If she kept walking, she could loop back up the other side of the golf course to Cypress Avenue and walk through Ocean Wood on her way home. It would be faster than retracing her steps.

Less than an hour later, she was back at Alexandra's

house, shivering as the sun set, and her hoodie did nothing to protect her from the damp fog rolling in.

Grok, still lounging on the front porch, jumped up and headed for the door when she arrived. Amanda could feel the waves of irritation coming from the cat.

He wanted to eat.

"I know. I'm sorry. It was so amazing to walk along the ocean. I got caught up." Amanda unlocked the door and went into the house.

The cat followed with a grumpy meow.

Not a Good Morning

Grok stared down at the sleeping form. He then smacked at it.

Amanda groaned and rolled over, the mattress making obscene squeaking noises that Grok found offensive.

And he hadn't been fed yet.

That seemed like provocation enough.

He'd also had to find a way into the van to her this morning. Fortunately, she had foolishly left the front doors unlocked.

But really, he didn't need any more reason than being unfed. He didn't like being forgotten.

Grok unsheathed a claw and held it high, then, with a quick slashing motion, sunk it deep into the mattress.

The hissing started low, then grew in volume as the woman floating on its surface sank. Eventually, the hissing stopped. The woman still hadn't moved.

Grok hesitated. If he revealed that he could talk to her, he could tell her exactly how unhappy he was with this situation. He wasn't ready to conclude testing but expressing his displeasure and getting fed would make the termination of the experiment worthwhile.

Amanda sat up, gasping. "What? Ouch, what happened to the mattress? Grok, did you do that?"

Grok had forgotten to pull back. She stared at his outstretched claw and then down at the very obvious hole in the blue material.

He put his claw away. He would wait for her outside.

Several minutes later, she stumbled, disheveled, out of the van, grumbling about the early hour and shaving cats.

He growled at the last comment. That was just mean. He hadn't been mean to her. He just wanted to expedite the situation—and get fed. In the back of his tattered mind, he was aware that in another life, he had been perfectly capable of getting himself fed, but that thought led to madness, and he pushed it back with a hiss.

"All right, I'm moving." She glared at him and then shuffled to unlock the door to the house.

Grok followed her to the kitchen, where she did something on the stove. He started to growl, but she opened the fridge and he rushed to his spot on the counter. She pulled several food packs out of the fridge to study.

He wanted to remind her that they were for eating, not for studying, but he was so close to his goal that he held his tongue.

Amanda held the packages up for display. "Would you like salmon, tuna, or beef for breakfast?"

Grok turned towards the first package with salmon.

Amanda returned the others to the fridge and then

hunted around in the drawers for something to open the package. With a yawn, she dumped a quarter of the container into the bowl with his name on it.

Grok growled softly.

She added a little bit more to the bowl and tutted. "The label says four servings per container. Just how much did my sister indulge you?"

Grok ignored her question and dove into the bowl.

Amanda returned the opened package to the fridge. She had several pressing concerns. Most importantly, what was she going to do with this cat? But also, how had the food gotten in the fridge? Could she ask the neighbors? Surely the police would find that reasonable. She would be staying out of the investigation. She could also do a little self-promotion at the same time and mention she was a groomer looking for work in case they knew anyone with an animal that needed her services.

Amanda scrunched up her nose. She hated the marketing side of the business. Give her an endless line of dirty dogs, and she is in heaven, but make her talk to potential customers, and she got all tongue-tied. But as she no longer had a veterinary clinic referring her, she better get used to talking.

With determination, Amanda made her breakfast, a package of instant oatmeal she found on the shelf and coffee. She treated herself to a shower in the house, dressed, then headed out.

Grok took up a protective position on the porch loveseat. Head back and eyes closed, the cat didn't move when Amanda locked the front door.

It was a beautiful day, the sun sharpening all the details wiped clean by morning dew and the sky an intense powder blue with big fluffy white clouds. As Amanda stepped off the porch, she sniffed the air like an addict, catching the hint of cool, crisp, salty air. She zipped her sweatshirt a little higher.

She planned to start at Dot's, but as she reached the sidewalk, she noticed Anh heading for his car across the street. She might as well get the worst one out of the way first.

"Hello?" Amanda called out. She had never met his wife, but she wished she could talk to her instead. She had to be friendlier than her husband. "I know you're busy. Do you have a few minutes to talk?"

Shoulders slumped under the fleece jacket, Anh slowly turned towards her. "What now?"

"I know you don't like me. I'm sorry for bothering you, but I'm trying to find out about caring for Grok. I found cat food in the fridge, and I was wondering if you had put it there?"

"I don't dislike you." Anh protested, not convincingly. His eyes shifted around as he avoided looking at her. "I've been sick lately, some stomach bug, and not acting like myself. I was also afraid you would tell someone about the RV."

At Amanda's confused look, the man continued. "I know you saw me yesterday and saw the parts the day before. Please don't tell my wife. She doesn't know I bought an RV. She won't be happy when she finds out." The man shuddered.

Amanda suddenly understood. He wasn't acting squirrelly because he killed someone. He was hiding his purchase from his wife.

Anh was wringing his hands as he continued. "I might have stretched the truth when I said the business was doing great. It's really the opposite." He gave a deep sigh and shrunk another inch. "Viktor wasn't renewing our lease, and we don't have the money to move. The business is probably going to fail. It's the worst possible time for me to buy an RV. But it was an amazing deal, and I couldn't pass it up. We've always talked about traveling America, and I thought, well if the business fails, we will have time..." the man's voice trailed off.

Now the secret was out into the open, Anh relaxed, and while his expression was still somber, his face had lost the pinched look, and his shoulders were no longer up by his ears.

"I had no idea. Don't worry. I won't say anything. I've never even met your wife."

"I'm going to tell her. I have to find the right time. As for your question, we weren't taking care of Grok. It must be someone else. You should ask Colleen. They weren't close, but they would pick up each other's mail sometime when the other was out of town. Mick, her husband, is a caterer and works long hours, but Colleen works from home and is there all the time, so Alexandra might've asked her."

Amanda thanked him for the information and promised she wouldn't say anything to his wife. Then she turned and headed across the street.

THIRTY-TWO

Secrets

Amanda knocked on Colleen's front door. No answer. Apparently, she was not home "all the time," as Anh had said. Amanda decided she would have to try again later, and she headed towards the next block and Dot's and Sally's houses.

In the spirit of tackling difficult calls first, Amanda passed Dot's house and opened the gate to Sally Walker's beautiful teal home. She knocked on the grey door and realized she wasn't sure what she was going to say to the woman. Since Amanda last spoke to her, Sally had learned her husband was dead.

Should she apologize? She did find his body.

Maybe she would just offer sympathy.

Sally never answered, so she never got to deliver her planned speech.

Instead of going back through the gate, she walked over to the woman's car. It was odd she was gone, but her car was here. The gravel crunched loudly under Amanda's feet. She glanced around, self-conscious of her snooping, then leaned in and looked in the back window of the SUV. Several large, open cardboard boxes labeled "Wildfire Victims Fundraiser" were in the back. They were full of camouflage gear, heavy hiking boots, and men's clothing. Were those Viktor's? Was Sally giving his things away so soon?

"Get away from my car." Sally's loud voice called out. She had another box in her hands and was locking the front door.

Amanda whirled around. Her prepared speech escaped her mind like a house cat when the door was left open, and she blurted out, "What are you doing? Are those Viktor's clothes?"

Sally glared at Amanda. "Don't you judge me? This is my grieving process." She threw the box she was holding into the back with the others and pushed past Amanda. Getting into the vehicle, she backed rapidly down the drive, clipping a fence post, then slammed the car into drive, and drove off.

"Still making friends, I see." Dot's laughter rang out, and Amanda saw her and Albert sitting on their front porch. "Come on over."

Amanda walked down the driveway to the sidewalk and headed to Dot's house, brushing by a big bushy plant with dramatic spears covered in trumpet-shaped purple flowers.

"She is giving all his things away." Amanda walked up

the steps to Dot's front porch and settled into a chair beside her.

"She is. We've been watching her pack up all day. She pulled her car into the garage for a while and we couldn't see what she loaded, but I suspect there is very little of Viktor's left in that house."

Amanda shook her head. But Sally was right, it wasn't hers to judge.

"Is that a weed? I see them everywhere." She pointed to the purple bush.

"Pride of Madeira. It's a shrub that thrives in this climate near the ocean with lots of sun. Hummingbirds love them." Albert's voice had a warble that made her think of a professor eager to impart the wisdom of a lifetime.

"It looks so alien. Everything looks so different here." Amanda felt disjointed.

"What happened at Sally's?" Dot poured her a cup of tea from the pot on the table.

Amanda hunched over the porcelain cup and breathed in the earthy blend of herbs. "I seem to be offending everyone today."

"Sometimes people are afraid of new or unfamiliar things. And you're new, and your van is very unfamiliar." Dot slapped her thigh at her joke and leaned back in laughter.

"Thanks for the philosophical support." Amanda studied the older woman. "You're always doing something new. Do they have a problem with you, too?"

Dot looked like she was thinking about it, then

shrugged. "Sometimes. I heard a lot of squawking when I took up racing. Then, sailing, scuba diving, and especially parasailing, everyone thought I was too old. They thought they knew everything about me, and it unsettled them I was doing something outside their comfortable understanding of who I was. But Bertie had my back and always has. Do you have someone that has your back?"

Amanda was startled but didn't have to think about the question. She shook her head.

"I see. Well, you're brave to be on this adventure." Dot took a sip of her tea.

Amanda's mind reeled at the idea. She had never considered trying to reconnect with her sister an adventure. Weren't adventures something you chose? When she had left her husband and was trying to figure out what came next, the desire to see Alexandra had become all-consuming. It was a need, an imperative, deep in her gut, that she had ignored for years. Now she was free, the calling took over. But she didn't seem to have a talent for finding lost people. She felt like she was just sitting here in this alien place with alien plants, waiting for something to happen.

"What can we help you with today?" Albert asked.

Amanda yearned for the kind of support Dot talked about. For that to happen, she had to start trusting someone.

So, she told Dot and Albert about finding Viktor's coat and someone trying to break into Alexandra's house. She also mentioned the cat food in the fridge.

Albert and Dot listened, nodding encouragingly.

When she was finished, Dot whistled. "Glad you're okay! What did the police find?"

"Nothing so far. They took photographs, but no one broke in, and nothing was taken. So, they couldn't do anything. But I'm not crazy, right? This is got to be related to Viktor's death?" Amanda sipped her tea, her brow wrinkled as her mind worked overtime.

"It seems a bit much for a coincidence." Dot crossed her arms and tapped a finger against her cheek as she thought. "Maybe you riled someone up, or they were looking for something. Ocean Wood is usually a safe town, in no small part thanks to your friend Chief Rodriguez."

Amanda choked. "Friend is stretching it."

"Okay, Alexandra's friend."

Amanda nodded.

Dot continued, "She's a smart woman. I trust her. Maybe you should, too."

Amanda thought about the notebook. Should she tell the chief about it?

Thinking of that, she had heard something this morning that was bothering her. "When I talked to Anh Nguyen, he mentioned he had been sick. And yesterday Frank said he had been sick too. Coincidence?"

Dot burst out laughing. She doubled over in her seat. When she could finally talk, she sat up, wiping her eyes. "Those crazy fools. They're in a mushroom foraging club. On hunt days, they go out at the crack of dawn, afraid someone will beat them to the best fungi. They spend the morning drinking thermoses of Irish coffee and wandering around collecting mushrooms and making up tales about the adventure. Then the drunk old farts come home and sleep it off so they can go out again in the afternoon to celebrate their finds at the Lighthouse, a pub in town. Normally, I'd say they just drank too much. But last time, one of the idiots made sandwiches to take out with them, and the whole lot came down with food poisoning. They were sick for days."

Amanda grimaced. She felt a little queasy talking about people being sick. "Who's in the group?"

"Oh, it's Frank, Anh. And all the guys from the mechanic's shop. They were so sick they had to close for days. Also, the bank manager, Pete. He barfed in the lobby. What a mess. Jill from the library goes, but she didn't get sick. Probably because she is gluten-free. Oh, and Viktor."

"Viktor was sick?"

"Must have been. Everyone else was."

Amanda wondered if Detective Kim knew about this. She asked a few more questions about Grok, but it was obvious Dot wasn't the one caring for the cat.

Feeling much better, Amanda was saying farewell to Dot and Albert when the police arrived next door.

Detective Kim got out of one of the squad cars. He was holding a piece of paper, and several officers waited behind him while he knocked on the door. "Sally Walker, we have a warrant to search this property."

When no one answered, Amanda expected them to leave. But instead, the officers fanned out and started inspecting the gardens and side yard.

"Found it." A young woman in uniform hurried back to the detective with a key.

The detective taped the warrant to the front door, unlocked it and went inside, followed by several other officers.

"Now, what do you suppose that is all about?" Dot's voice held more than a hint of excitement, and she settled back in her chair for the show.

THIRTY-THREE

Hand-spun Art

Amanda stayed a few more minutes to see if she could learn anything while watching the police, but they were being discreet. Finally, she said goodbye to Dot and left.

Had talking to Dot about her suspicions been a mistake? She liked the woman and hoped she wasn't a murderess.

Almost back to her sister's house, Amanda heard someone call out her name. It was so unusual for someone not to mistake her for Alexandra she spun around, looking for the voice. The street was quiet, with only a few people out.

"Hello Amanda, do you have a minute?" Colleen stood on her front porch, waving a hand.

The woman had been so discombobulated and standoffish the first time they met Amanda was curious as to what she wanted. "Sure. How are you?"

"I'm good today. It's been a rough week. I wanted to

talk to you about Grok." Colleen stepped back into the house and held the door open for her.

Amanda hesitated on the sidewalk, confused by Colleen's flip-flops in attitude towards her. Maybe Dot was right that being the new person in town made people nervous. Amanda followed Colleen into her house.

The house's exterior was a mishmash of vibrant colors and textures, and the interior matched. Every wall was a different color, many of them with hand-painted murals. Woven cloth and beautiful textures hung from walls— some quilted, some knotted, each a work of art.

"Come on through to the sunroom. I cleared some space in there." Amanda followed Colleen into a room at the back of the house. It was identical to Alexandra's sunroom but buzzed with energy from all the color and incomplete projects. Light flooded in from the sunlight above and the windows on three sides of the room. A light morning breeze wafted in through a propped open window. Amanda would never tire of smelling the hint of ocean in the air.

"What a lovely room!" Amanda exclaimed. She walked over to look out the back and appreciate the view of the small garden.

"Thank you. It's one of my favorite rooms in the house. My studio has similar lighting but not the same view of the garden. What can I get you to drink?"

"Anything is fine." Amanda wandered the room while Colleen poured two cups of coffee. "Did you do this?" Amanda pointed to a series of wildflower paintings over a fireplace.

"Yes, a few years ago. My plant phase. Then there was a life drawing phase," Colleen pointed to a large portrait of a nude woman hanging in the next room. "Then my pottery phase," Colleen picked up the two mugs and handed one to Amanda. "And my jewelry phase," she shook her head, and her earrings tinkled. "I'm into landscapes now and knitting. My paintings are selling pretty well in the gallery in town." She placed her mug on the table, and Colleen indicated Amanda should sit, then sat across from her.

Amanda was impressed. She'd never known an artist popular enough to sell her paintings. She asked several questions about her work, and Colleen became animated as they chatted.

Amanda noticed a skein of hand-spun pink and green wool with a half-completed knitting project in a basket by the table. "Hey, that's the same wool as Alexandra's hat. You must have made it. I've been wearing the hat. It's so soft and warm."

Colleen's eyes grew comically large. She took a big gulp of her coffee and choked. Amanda was stuck in a strange place where she didn't know a person well enough to lend a comforting hand but also didn't want to call an ambulance if it wasn't necessary. "Are you okay?"

"About Grok," the woman gasped and cleared her throat.

"The fridge was restocked with cat food when I got home yesterday. It was unsettling. Do you know who is feeding the cat?"

"I am so sorry. It was me. Alexandra asked me to take care of Grok. Not that the cat requires much care, but you don't want to see what will happen if dinner is late." Colleen had regained her breath and blew out a puff. Her bangs ruffled like grass in the wind. She got up and went to a box on the mantelpiece, pulling out a key. "The cat food is on auto-ship. When it arrived yesterday, I saw it on the porch, let myself in, and put it away. I should've told you I had a key. I didn't mean to scare you. I'm so sorry."

Amanda was stunned by the admission. At least that mystery was solved. "It's okay. I'm relieved. I thought my sister had come back. And I must admit I was worried she was mixed up with everything that happened to Viktor."

Colleen froze at the mention of Viktor's name, but when Amanda didn't follow up with a question about the man, she slowly relaxed again.

The conversation faltered after that. The back-and-forth flow between them gone. Amanda was disappointed. Colleen was interesting and funny, and she enjoyed talking about her art.

She said her goodbyes and left.

As she was walking home, Amanda suddenly remembered Alexandra didn't like hats. Hated them. Would refuse to wear them on even the coldest snowy day in Ohio. There was no way the pink and green hat she found on top of the casebook was Alexandra's. It must have been Colleen's. She must have been in the house when Amanda arrived and found Viktor. She was the killer!

Amanda had to tell Ben. No, she had to tell Detective Kim. She considered calling but was afraid to stop anywhere near Colleen's house. What if she saw her? What if she followed her?

She reached the Pink Pup and unlocked the side door. She looked around. No one was watching. She grabbed the hat and shoved it under her sweatshirt until it looked like she had a third boob, and put the casebook in her purse. Then she locked up the van and started strolling towards town. She tried to look casual as she walked as fast as she could to the police station.

THIRTY-FOUR

Baked Goods & Boots

Amanda wouldn't say she ran all the way to the police station, but by the time she was standing outside Ben's office, she had sweat streaking down her face and was panting. Hands-on her knees, she was hauling air into her lungs when Ben found her.

"Amanda, what's wrong?" He rushed to her side and put an arm across her back to help support her.

"I'm okay, just catching my breath." When Amanda could straighten, she reached under her sweatshirt and pulled out the hat.

"What's that, and why was it in your shirt?" Ben eyed the pink and green yarn.

"I didn't want anyone, especially Colleen, to see I had it." Amanda started to feel foolish. It was a hat, not a smoking gun. "This might have been a mistake."

"No, come on. I want to help. Tell me what is going on." Ben nodded to the hat without taking it.

Amanda dropped her arm and started explaining about finding the hat and the casebook, about the mushroom tart on the first morning, about trying to decipher the code in the book, about everyone on the mushroom foraging trip getting sick, and about finding out that the hat was Colleen's. By the time she was done, she was waving the cap around and pacing back and forth in front of Ben.

Ben narrowed his eyes and pulled a pair of gloves from his pocket. He put them on and took the hat.

"This was in the house when you arrived?" He asked.

Amanda nodded.

"With the casebook?" He clarified.

She nodded again.

"Wait, did you say you received an anonymous *mushroom* tart?"

Amanda nodded again.

Ben paled. He pulled out his phone with his other hand and struggled to dial the number one-handed, his gloved fingers sticking to the case.

A woman answered the phone. "Sorry, Mother, wrong number. I'll call you later and explain." He hung up on her mid-sentence and dialed again. He hung up. "Nope, that's my landlord."

Finally, Amanda pulled the phone from his hand. "Who are you trying to call?"

"Detective Kim."

Amanda scrolled to the number, dialed, and returned the phone to Ben. The two men spoke briefly, and Ben hung up.

"He's on his way. You'll have to repeat the whole story for him."

"You don't think I'm overreacting?" Amanda's tone was hopeful.

Ben shook his head. "The labs came back. A death cap mushroom poisoned Viktor Walker. You are lucky to be alive."

Amanda couldn't believe it. She felt a little dizzy. She leaned forward again, then squatted down, her elbows on her knees. Ben crouched beside her and put his arm back around her waist.

"What have you got?" Detective Kim jogged down the hallway to them. Amanda noted he wasn't out of breath.

Ben stood up to greet the man. Briefly explained and handed her off to the detective while he processed the new evidence. As he left, Ben reminded her, "We are cleaning tonight, and I'm bringing dinner. No tarts."

Amanda nodded and warned, "I'm definitely off baked goods for a while."

Ben chuckled as he headed back into his lab.

She followed Detective Kim back to his office and made a brief statement about what had happened. "Can I keep the casebook?"

The detective shook his head and held out a hand for the book. "You shouldn't have removed it from the house. But we are no longer considering the house the primary scene. We think he was poisoned somewhere else, probably at home, maybe even by his own hand, and then went to Alexandra's house and got sick. Let me talk to the chief about the casebook and see if we can clear it."

"Do you think all the foragers got sick from the poison mushroom, and only Viktor died?" Amanda shivered.

"Maybe. But they would probably all be dead if they had eaten death cap. They said Viktor liked to cook with what he found in the woods. Maybe he made the pastry and took it to the house, leaving it where you found it the next morning."

Amanda was never going to eat something she found in the forest. As she gathered up her things, she asked, "Is it safe to go back to the house?"

"We are going to send someone to question Colleen. Just stay out of her way for now."

Amanda didn't know how she felt about that and was glad Ben would be coming over that evening.

They stepped out of the building. "Take care, Amanda, and don't eat any food you don't know where it came from." The man turned to leave.

"Wait," Amanda called, and Detective Kim turned back to her with a raised eyebrow. "There was something else. I didn't want you to think I was snooping, but I was at Sally Walker's house and saw she was donating boxes of clothing and kitchen stuff. This was before you went there with the warrant. I thought it was suspicious."

"But you weren't snooping?" The stern voice came from behind her.

Amanda grimaced. She turned around to see an annoyed Chief Rodriguez with a to-go cup in one hand.

"It's good information, chief. We suspected the house had been cleaned out. Now we have it confirmed." The detective defended Amanda.

"At what price? I got a call someone might have tried to poison you. You are not your sister. You need to leave the investigations to professionals, or when your sister returns, I'll have to explain why I had you removed from her property. Do you understand?" The chief glared at her.

Amanda steamed at being talked to like a child, but she nodded.

Then the chief went into the building, followed by the detective.

Amanda leaned a hand against the side of the building, her fingers biting into the white stone. Her legs were trembling. The chief was right. But did she know more about her sister's disappearance than she let on?

Shaking off the experience, she took a deep breath and resolved to stop snooping and let the police handle it.

She had other things to consider now, like what was happening with that cat and why she felt like a science experiment.

Amanda was so distracted on the walk home that she would have walked into a cypress tree if someone hadn't shouted at her.

What now? She searched around until she saw the young woman storming towards her, blond hair flapping like a wave as she dragged a pair of yipping Chihuahuas on pink diamond studded leashes behind her.

"You! I know what you did." She pointed a long, bejeweled fingernail at Amanda. The woman was fuming. It took a minute for Amanda to remember who she was. It was the woman who worked in the Best Friends Boutique when she was dropping off business cards.

"I remember you, but I don't know your name—" Amanda left the sentence open, hoping for an introduction. Instead, she received a withering glare that would have melted metal.

"I don't know your game, but I was here first." Her words were each punctuated by a nail jab into the air. "These are my clients, not yours. You best mind your own business or else."

The young woman flicked the wave of glossy hair over her shoulder and stormed off. Trailing the barking Chihuahuas behind her.

Amanda added the experience to her list of weird things that had happened that day.

Soon after she turned on Lily Street, she became aware that it was busier than it should be. People were out of their homes, staring down the street—at Alexandra's house.

No, not Alexandra's house. It was the house next door.

Amanda joined Frank in his driveway. "What's going on?"

"Don't know. The police just turned up. Detective Kim went into Colleen's house with another officer. Then a couple more officers went around back."

Amanda stared at the house where she had had coffee that morning and tried not to make eye contact with Frank in case he asked questions she couldn't answer.

"You wouldn't believe what I just heard." Anh walked up next to them. His fleece jacket had been swapped for an unzipped fleece vest over a t-shirt. "I heard they are searching Colleen's house."

"You don't say." Frank turned to Anh and gave him an annoyed stare. "All you have to do is look across the street to know that. What good are your contacts in the police department if you don't know more than we can figure out with our own eyes?"

Just then, Detective Kim escorted Colleen from the house. Her hands were behind her back.

"Is she wearing handcuffs?" Amanda had never seen anyone arrested before.

Frank looked surprised.

If Colleen had poisoned Vik, why had she tried to poison Amanda? She had never met the woman at that point.

Officer Hartman came out next, holding a pair of colorful boots in his gloved hands. He added them to the items they were taking from the house as evidence.

"Hey, those look like my boots that were stolen." Frank revved up, ready to stomp over and confront the police.

"Are you sure they are yours?" Anh asked.

"How many pairs of rainbow-colored Wellingtons have you seen?" Frank's tone implied he couldn't understand why he was asking such a stupid question.

Anh tapped Frank kindly on the arm for the insult and said, "Just checking because if those are evidence, you might not want to admit they're yours."

Frank looked stunned. "Well, they might not be mine."

The three watched as the police came in and out with

several boxes of items. Eventually, they started wrapping up the search.

Realizing the time, Amanda said goodbye to the neighbors and headed to the Pink Pup to set up for the show dog Bonny's grooming appointment.

THIRTY-FIVE

Dinner

Ben arrived just as Amanda was finishing feeding Grok dinner. The cat had followed her into the house from the porch when she offered to give him an early dinner.

Amanda opened the front door for Ben. He wore the same button-down shirt she had seen him in a few hours ago, buttoned to his chin, with grey dress pants and sneakers. But his hair was smoothed back. He looked nice.

Why had she never noticed he wore sneakers to work? She was being ridiculous. Of course, he had come straight from work. She had only changed because she was worried her other shirt might smell like Bonny, the dog.

His arms were laden with bags of PPE gear, cleaning equipment, and, from the smell, Thai food.

"I've got the vacuum in the truck. I'll go get it after we eat."

Amanda grabbed an armload to help. "Where should we put this down?"

"Did you already clean the kitchen?" He pushed down the hood of the protective suit in her arms to see her nod. "Then, let's set up in there."

Ben followed her into the kitchen.

"Hey, can you help me board up the window before we eat?" Amanda pointed to a cut piece of plywood she had found in the shed, along with nails and a hammer.

Ben crouched down in front of the door to examine the window. "Sure, but it's a small puncture. Just the one pane. We could use some tape and plastic bags to seal it."

"Will that be secure?" Amanda had been worried about damaging the door with a larger fix, so this sounded better.

"It will be watertight. If they are going to break in again, they could do it at any window." Ben got up and grabbed thick gloves from his PPE bag.

Amanda found sturdy tape and black trash bags under the counter. She handed the tools to Ben, and he made quick work of the fix. She breathed easier when it was done.

"So, tell me about your day," Amanda asked as she spread the food out on the kitchen table. Ben told her about the escapades of the medical examiner's office. She was in stitches when he finished the story about his new assistants at their first autopsy.

"How did they get the job with no experience?" Amanda gasped around a laugh.

"No idea." Ben shook his head. "I'm not sure they are going to make the cut."

Amanda switched topics. "So, I'm assuming you've heard about Colleen?"

"No, what happened? Ben asked.

Amanda was surprised; she thought the police department kept each other appraised and said as much.

"I'm not part of the police department, remember. It's very unusual that I'm in Ocean Wood so many days a week."

"Why are you here so often? I thought you said you would spend most of your time in Salinas." Amanda asked.

"Wily, Chief Rodriguez can be thanked for that. She had space for a facility here and managed to finagle funds for my two assistants from the county budgets and hired them locally. So, I am based most of the week at the Ocean Wood office. I'm finding I don't mind. It's beautiful. Do you know how hot it gets in Salinas? While it's 70 degrees here, Salinas spends most of the summer over 90 degrees." Ben swept a dramatic hand over his forehead as he sank back against the counter.

"Will it ever get that hot here?" Hot, muggy summers were normal for Amanda, and she knew how to dress for them. She was having more trouble figuring out the weather on the Monterey Peninsula. No matter what she wore, she was always over-dressed or freezing.

"No, hardly ever. Ocean Wood's weather is like San Francisco's. The fog and breeze off the ocean keep it cool. It'll pull even more fog off the ocean when it gets hot in the valley. It can get pretty thick."

Amanda couldn't imagine it worse than it had been.

"Now, what happened with Colleen? She's the one that lives over there, right?" Ben waved a hand towards Colleen's house.

Amanda nodded. "It looked like she was arrested today. They searched her house and took in several boxes of stuff as evidence. Frank says he saw his stolen boots in what they removed from the house."

"His boots?" While Ben was waiting for the rest of the story, he took the forks and plates from her and added them to the table, then pulled out her chair.

Ben dumped half the Pra Ram Tofu on his plate and most of the rice, then doused it in more peanut sauce.

"Fan of peanut sauce?" Amanda teased.

"Love it. That's why I got two containers. Here, try it with the Pad Thai." He held out two containers to her and asked about her work.

Amanda told him about Buddy, the beautiful golden retriever she had groomed yesterday, and Bonny today. And about their owner, Katrina, flirting with Detective Kim.

Ben laughed. "His dating is kind of notorious in the department. On my first day, they told me about a woman he met at a bar and decided he would be cool and invite her to run with him. He is pretty proud of his speed. Well, she was a Major going to the Naval Postgraduate School and a much faster runner than him, record-breaking fast. He was so shocked he tripped, broke his nose, and they spent the date in the ER getting it reset."

Amanda snorted, then slapped a hand over her mouth.

She would forever think of that story now when she saw the detective.

"Oh, I met this angry woman who works at the Best Friends Boutique today. Well, I met her yesterday, but today, she chased after me and accused me of stealing. I don't understand why she is so upset with me." Amanda twirled noodles around her fork but didn't lift them to her mouth.

"I can tell you that. I haven't been here long, but I looked for a groomer first off. I went to my Best Friend's Boutique and found out that Chloe, her name, is the only groomer in town."

"She's a groomer? How does she do it with those nails?"

"No idea. She works part-time in the boutique and rents a room in the back for grooming. Qbert wouldn't let her near him. That's part of why he was in such a mess when you saw him."

"But Qbert is a dear. Very easy to work with." Amanda protested.

Ben smiled. "Maybe for you."

"Ben, how long have you and Qbert been in town?" Amanda asked.

"A couple weeks. I found a furnished hotel room that took dogs and grabbed it. Eventually, I'll look for something different. But I want things settled at work first."

"And is it settling down?" Amanda spurred on.

"Not yet, but it sure is getting interesting. Death Cap poisoning that isn't accidental—that rarely happens."

Amanda could tell Ben was trying to suppress the glee. She had to admit medical examiners had a weird job.

"Death caps mushrooms are found locally?" It made Amanda queasy to think about how close she had come to eating that tart.

"Yes. They can be found throughout this area. You do get occasional cases of poisoning. But rarely is it used for murder. It's a particularly brutal way to die."

"So, it was a murder," Amanda said.

Ben bobbled his head from side to side, uncommitted, before he continued. "Then there are those footprints between your house, Colleens, and the victims. I'm not surprised they brought her in. Course, they also found the bottle of dried mushrooms at her house. We are still testing those. Oh, shoot. I wasn't going to tell you that."

"What?" Amanda gasped. "Dried mushrooms? And someone was outside all three houses? Are you kidding me? Hey, I thought you didn't know about Colleen!"

"They just brought the dried mushrooms and the hair dye to me for testing so we could compare it to the victim's results. I didn't know about other evidence or that anyone had been arrested."

"Hair dye?"

"Oh shoot, I wasn't supposed to mention that either." Ben put his head in his hands, elbows on the table.

"Come on, what else do you know I should know." Amanda didn't want Ben to get into trouble, but some of this was important for her to know for her safety.

"Well, the most important thing is that they found boot prints outside your front window and all around the house and leading to and from Colleen's house. That's why I was checking which side her house was on. And they found prints leading to and from Viktor Walker's house. And there was also evidence of a break-in at Viktor's house. They think Colleen broke in and poisoned something he was going to eat. But they're still not sure why."

Amanda reached across the table and grabbed Ben's arm. "The affairs!"

THIRTY-SIX

Secret Room

At Ben's raised brow, Amanda continued. "Katrina said Vik was known for pressuring women into sleeping with him. I was worried it might be my sister. But maybe it was Colleen?"

"That's awful." Ben's forehead creased. He put down his fork. "We'll see what happens when they question her."

Amanda had lost her appetite.

Those three houses were very close together. Someone could easily move between them and not be seen. Amanda had thought it was a grass stain on Vik's hand, but it was such a vivid green that hair dye made much more sense.

"Hey, try to finish your dinner." Ben nudged her hand with his, and he resumed eating.

After several minutes of picking at her food, she finally gave up and pushed her plate away. Ben finished his dish and sat back in his chair with a smile. "That was delicious. Ready to get to work?"

Amanda's phone rang. She ignored it and collected the plates instead.

Ben gave her a curious look. "Aren't you going to answer that?"

Amanda shook her head. At Ben's frown, she pulled out her phone, but the call had already gone to voice mail.

She showed him the screen. "Oops. Missed it."

"Hey, what is that?" Ben said at the same time. He grabbed the phone and showed her the picture on the screen of the two of them in the kitchen holding a phone. Then, the image slid to one from the porch and one from the backyard. "I didn't know there were cameras here."

"Is that what those are? The images have been randomly coming up whenever I get on my phone. It started happening when I signed on to the network." Amanda studied one of the images. Grok was stretched the full length of the couch, taking a power nap.

"How did you get the guest password?" Ben was looking over her shoulder. When the picture of them in the kitchen came back on the screen, he grabbed the phone, "Excuse me." He said over his shoulder as he waved his hand and walked to a corner. Pointing up at the wall, suddenly, "Ah, ha, gotcha! There is the camera, see it? That black dot the size of a quarter?"

Hiding in the wallpaper pattern, Amanda could see it. She shivered. Creeped out to know she'd been on camera and didn't know it. "Oh, that's what happened." She grabbed Ben's arm. "I didn't log on with a guest password. I recognized the network name and used my sister's favorite saying for the password. The network thinks I am her. That's why I'm getting all these images."

"It's probably set to go off when there is motion in the house. Do you know where the hardware is? The server?"

Amanda shook her head, but her face lit up. "You are right! Each camera probably has its own storage, but if the network is sending me images from all of them, they might be networked and backed up together. That's how the system worked that I set up at my ex's veterinary clinic."

"That would explain it. Have you searched the whole house?" Ben handed back her phone.

"Yes, but there was a locked door in the hallway I couldn't get into."

"Well, let's go look," Ben grabbed Amanda's hand and pulled her out of the kitchen.

Amanda tripped at the feel of his warm fingers twining with hers. She righted herself and took over, directing them to the door. "You gonna break it down?"

"Oh, ha-ha, I happen to be fairly good at picking locks." At her raised brow, Ben released her hand and straightened his imaginary tie.

Amanda grabbed the knob of the closet door and twisted it to show it was locked. The handle turned, and the door swung open.

"What? I swear that was locked yesterday." Amanda shivered.

"Well, let's check it out."

Amanda reached in and, with trembling fingers, patted the wall, looking for a switch. There was nothing.

Behind her, Ben turned on his phone's flashlight and

pointed it over the room. The large furnace closet had a dry, musty smell and was empty of anything besides the mechanical unit. He pushed into the gap on the other side of the furnace and swung the light around the bare space.

"What's that?"

"What's what?" Ben scanned the floor to see what he had missed.

"Look up." Amanda squeezed in next to Ben and pointed to the ceiling.

The light caught on a gap between a trap door and the ceiling.

"Hold this." Ben handed off his phone and then jumped. With the tips of his fingers, he caught the edge of the door and pulled.

As the door opened, a folding attic stair slid out, almost spearing them in the chest in the small space. They split up, each standing flush to an opposite wall, and the ladder slid down between them.

Amanda held the phone closer to the opening, but it didn't permeate the thick darkness at the top of the ladder. "We are going to have to go up. Follow me."

Slowly, Amanda crept up the stairs, holding the rungs with one hand. Head above the opening, she waved her light around. She could see a low-ceiling room with boxes but not much more. She finished climbing the stairs and pulled herself up through the hatch.

"What is all this?" Ben pulled himself into the attic room behind her.

With her head brushing the beams as she walked. The only light in the room coming from a small white box.

"If Alexandra installed this, she must have suspected something was going on in the house when she was gone." Ben crouched beside the blinking light. "We need to call Detective Kim. Maybe he can make sense of this."

Amanda nodded her head in agreement. She handed back Ben's phone so he could make the call.

THIRTY-SEVEN

Cameras Off

The police turned up much quicker this time. Detective Kim's face was grim as he surveyed the attic.

"Did you touch anything?"

In her head, Amanda retraced her steps into the attic. "No?"

Detective Kim raised an eyebrow at her.

Ben left the officer he was talking to and walked hunched over to them. "I think someone came in while she was gone. Amanda said the door was locked when she checked it yesterday."

The police detective nodded. He ducked under a beam and waited until the photographer had taken photos, then examined the network box with a gloved hand. "It looks intact. Why don't you two wait downstairs for us? Officer Hartman will show you the way."

The officer watched them like a cat tracking prey as they returned down the stairs and out to the living room.

It creeped Amanda out to know a camera was watching them while they sat there.

"I'm so glad I'm not sleeping in here."

"Yeah, me too. I guess we will have to clean up another night. Can I leave all the equipment here?" Ben pointed the direction of the kitchen.

"You won't need them?"

"No, those are my personal cleaning supplies. I have a heavy-duty version for work." Ben replied.

Amanda choked back a laugh, imagining Ben cleaning his apartment in full hazmat gear.

"I'm going to grab my purse from the kitchen and make sure all the food is put away." Amanda left Ben on the sofa, checking his email. She was returning to the living room when Detective Kim walked in.

"Oh, that is interesting," Ben muttered.

"What is it, doc?" The detective asked, leaning against the wall by the front door.

"The additional toxicology reports I ordered came in. Most likely, Viktor ingested the poison mushroom on the 18th. Something threw off my estimate." Ben frowned.

Amanda stood up from where she was leaning over her bag. "If everyone on his mushroom foraging trip had been sick, would food poisoning change how the death caps affected him?"

"It's possible he ingested the mushroom and didn't recognize the symptoms because of the food poisoning. Otherwise, an experienced forager like him would have known something was happening."

The detective sighed. "Well, that clears the wife. She

was definitely with family in LA. They were at an all-day sports event for the grandkids. Then she went shopping, and they saw her again in the evening. She didn't come back to town until two days later."

Detective Kim turned to Amanda. "Where were you on the 18th of the month?"

Amanda thought back. It seemed so long ago. *Oh.* Her head sank. "I was in Arizona."

"Do you have a receipt or something that proves this?" The detective studied her blushing face.

"Worse. The Pink Pup got a flat tire, and while I was trying to get it changed, people started stopping by and taking selfies. There are at least thirty pictures of people with the truck. It's all online on social media. I'm in the background of a few of them."

Detective Kim stifled a snort.

Ben wasn't so discreet and rolled sideways on the couch as he howled with laughter.

Amanda hugged her arms to her chest. "So, it was Colleen?"

"There's more." Ben gasped and held up a hand as he caught his breath. Then he put on his professional face and added, "The glass bottle did contain a dry death cap. There were no fingerprints on the jar."

Detective Kim looked grim. "Looks like I'm heading back to Colleen's house to check her kitchen equipment. The officers are wrapping up here. You're free to stay in the house if you want to."

At the look on Amanda's face, the detective shrugged. "Or just tell me where you are going so, we know where to find you. The officers can lock up after they are done."

"I'll be here, but I'll sleep out in the Pink Pup. Are the cameras off?" Amanda picked up her bag and put it over her shoulder.

"Yes, we've removed all the equipment and are taking it in for evidence. All the cameras we found on the outside had missing memory cards. I suspect they were removed." The detective nodded his head at her and left.

"It's just so creepy." Amanda couldn't help exclaiming.

Ben nodded in agreement. "Ready to go?"

Ben walked her out to the Pink Pup. "You sure you'll be OK in here?"

"Absolutely. I feel safer already."

Ben nodded and turned to go. Amanda stopped him. "Ben, can you think of anything we have found that ties one of my sister's cases to Viktor's death?"

Ben looks surprised.

Amanda continued, "I found Alexandra's private investigator's casebook when I first entered the house. I turned it in to Detective Kim, but he hasn't given it back. It's written in code, and I've been trying to decipher it. I haven't figured it out yet."

"What did Detective Kim say?" Ben leaned in.

"That I shouldn't have removed it from the house." Amanda relaxed against the side of the Pink Pup. Was that the problem? She was trying to find a relationship between the casebook and Vik's death. Maybe there wasn't any.

Ben tilted his head to the side and thought for a minute. "I'm not seeing the connection to the case."

"Thanks, that's what I thought, too, but I needed a second opinion." Amanda gave him a grateful look.

Ben smiled at her. "Well, you can always ask me. I'm happy to help. Good night."

Amanda watched as Ben got into his jeep and drove off. The police were still finishing up in the house, so she climbed into the Pink Pup, shut the door, and set up her bed for the night like she had many nights before.

As Grok settled in on the on the front seat of Amanda's pink monster of a vehicle, he had an unsettled feeling. Should he have told Amanda about the cameras? And exactly how would he do that without ending the experiment and revealing his secret? He could point at the ceiling. Pantomime being caught unaware. Draw arrows in the dirt to the location of the hidden camera that the police hadn't found and removed. Any one of those actions might result in more attention than he wanted.

Amanda had only been here a couple of days, and he didn't feel he should betray all of Alexandra's secrets. When she returned, she could decide whether to tell her sister everything. For now, Grok was committed to keeping them both alive and fed.

He rolled to his back and even as he squirmed in the uncomfortable seat, he felt his eyes start to sag. *Worst guard cat ever*, whispered through his mind as he fell asleep.

THIRTY-EIGHT

The Attack

A low growl woke Amanda. It was pitch black, and for a minute, she wasn't sure where she was. Then she felt the sleeping bag around her and the flattened air mattress beneath her and remembered that she was in the Pink Pup.

What time was it? She searched for her phone and found it was just before 3 AM.

The growl sounded again. Amanda recognized the threatening sound coming from Grok. "Where are you?" She called to the cat.

A low guttural meow came from the front cab of the vehicle. Was Grok trying to get in? Or out? She couldn't remember if he had stayed in the house or followed her into the van last night.

Amanda crawled out of the sleeping bag and put on her shoes using her phone as a flashlight and headed for the door that separated the cab from the rest of the van. She was opening the door when she heard a noise outside. A metal scratching along the side panel. Amanda turned her head, following the sound from the inside as it brushed down the side of the van.

Someone was out there.

Grok hissed as he rushed in and ran to the back of the van, where Amanda had heard the scratching noise.

"What is it?" Amanda waited for an answer. She sniffed and screwed up her nose. Why did the air smell like burnt rubber?

Quickly searching around for a weapon, she grabbed the tools she was most familiar with, shoving the wireless electric hair trimmer into her front pocket and holding her sharpened scissors before her like a knife.

Grok padded to the side door and swiped a paw at it, catching the handle. The door would've opened if Amanda hadn't locked it last night. Holding the scissors in the same hand as her phone, she struggled to unlock the door with one hand.

Amanda batted Grok's paw off the handle, unlocked it, and slid open the door.

Grok shot outside.

She scrambled to follow the cat to the front of the vehicle.

Pale moonlight lit the front of the van. There was nothing there. But the smell of burnt rubber increased, and a light flickered from the far side. Amanda kept walking, her hand shaking as she stuck her head around the side.

In the dark, orangish-red embers glowed and crackled.

It took a second for Amanda to see the piles of leaves and debris shoveled against the van and set on fire.

And whoever had done it was still there.

Amanda watched as Grok launched at the dark figure. The figure dropped the end of the rag they were holding, but one end was already on fire—the other fed into the gas tank.

"I've called the police. You better get out of here." Amanda's bluff didn't work.

The figure turned towards her and hissed, "Give me your phone!"

The dark form rushed her, and Amanda stumbled back, dropping the scissors.

Amanda spun away from the vehicle as flames from the burning debris leaped up to the fuzzy ears on the side of the van. Running, as she headed for the porch, she yelled for help.

"Fire! Fire—" Her shout was stopped as arms wrapped around her chest and yanked her back toward the flames.

Instinctively, Amanda reached for her next weapon, grabbing the electric trimmer in her pocket; she flicked it on and threw her arm back, trying to hit the person who held onto her.

There was a loud yelp behind her and a shearing sound as the trimmer made contact. The arms around her chest loosened, and Amanda pulled away, only to have the hands transfer to her throat.

"This wouldn't be happening if your sister hadn't interfered with my plan." A woman's voice screeched in Amanda's ear.

"Alexandra didn't do anything!" Amanda gasped out.

"Give. Me. That. Phone!" The woman shook her with each word.

Amanda threw her hand back behind her head again. The trimmers made contact once more with something soft. The intruder shrieked.

Amanda was flung to the ground.

"Watch out." Shouted Grok.

Stunned, Amanda hesitated. Had Grok just spoken to her? She'd felt and heard the words in her head. How was that possible?

She felt the rush of an attack and rolled.

Razor-sharp scissors stabbed into the ground where her face had been. For a second, she was face to face with Sally Walker. Then the woman screamed and stabbed again.

"He was having an affair. Nobody does that to me. But I taught him a lesson. And now you are going to get yours."

Amanda rolled in the other direction. Turning, she could see the moonlight flash on metal as the arm raised again and came towards her.

Suddenly, the arc changed trajectory as Sally gave an agonized scream and jerked around.

Grok had latched on to the attacker's back. The nails of all four paws were deeply embedded through the jacket into her skin.

Sally screamed and whirled like a top. Trying to rip the cat off her back, she stabbed with the scissors.

The figure finally lunged backward, slamming Grok into the side of the burning van.

"No!" Amanda scrambled to her feet.

Grok released the prey. The acrid smell of burnt hair joined the pungent aroma of smoldering rubber and leaves as the cat slid to the ground.

Amanda was relieved to see Grok rolling away from the fire.

Sally wasn't as lucky; her coat caught fire, and in a frenzy of motion, she tried to put out the flames. Her figure bobbed and weaved. Arms flailing, she ran away from the van, smacking into the side of the house.

There was a loud *thunk* as Sally's head hit the wood siding. She froze, then slowly fell backward, unconscious. The rolling body extinguished the flames.

Amanda scrambled towards Grok, but the cat was already on his feet, sniffing the intruder for any sign of movement.

The figure was still.

"Amanda, are you okay?" Frank raced across the street, a fire extinguisher in his hands.

She called out that she was fine, and Frank immediately started spraying the side of the van, pulling the burning rag out of the gas tank just in time.

Feeling very strange, Amanda tried coordinating her limbs to grab the hose at the side of the house. She had to kick aside a pile of leaves and old rags that had been pushed up against the wooden porch. They stank of gasoline.

Feeling woozy, she stumbled as she leaned over to turn on the water. Bracing against the side of the house, she turned the hose on the intruder. When she was convinced those flames were out, she pointed the hose at the van.

They had the flames extinguished by the time the fire trucks rolled up.

The police were right behind.

Amanda looked around to check on Grok. The cat was standing guard over their unconscious intruder.

Officer Hartman was the first on the scene.

Amanda directed him to the intruder. "She started the fire."

The officer scowled down at the unconscious woman. "It's Sally Walker!"

Exhausted, Amanda turned off the hose and attempted to lower herself to the ground. "She just tried to kill me, and she killed her husband." Amanda's trembling legs gave out, and she ended up sitting in the bushes. Resigned, she leaned back against the house and closed her eyes.

THIRTY-NINE

Hair Cut

"Amanda?"

She cracked open an eye and stared at Detective Kim, who was motioning a paramedic over. "Check Amanda out. Make sure she's not injured."

"Your killer, Sally Walker, is over there." Amanda waved her hand in the direction where she had last seen Grok guarding the woman.

"No, she's getting checked out in the ambulance, like you should be. Then you can tell me what's going on here." The detective didn't listen to her protests and, when the paramedic gave the okay, helped Amanda to her feet.

She leaned heavily into the detective. Maybe she did need to get looked at.

"You have someone watching her, right?" Amanda was too weary to look.

"Officer Hartman is keeping an eye on her. Did Sally Walker really set fire to your van?" Detective Kim studied the vehicle in the drive.

"Where is Grok, is he okay? He saved my life!" Amanda searched around for the cat.

"He is right over there with the vet." The detective assured her.

The fire department had arrived in time to move the brush away from the van, putting out the last of the embers.

One of the firefighters walked up to Detective Kim. "We did a preliminary search. The fire is out in all locations. The damage to the van appears to be cosmetic. Luckily, it didn't blow. All those fumes on an empty tank are more dangerous than if it had been full."

Amanda's eyes widened, and the firefighter continued. "There wasn't any damage to the house. We dispersed several ignition points around the building. It's all clear now."

"The house?" Amanda sank down. An EMT came up beside her and scooped an arm around her waist, guiding her to the back of a second ambulance. They checked her vitals and looked her over for burns. Amanda was okay, just exhausted after the adrenaline rush of the fight.

"Okay, now why don't you tell me what happened?" Detective Kim moved to her side.

Suddenly, the woman in the next ambulance saw Amanda. A scream emerged from Sally Walker, and she lunged for Amanda. "Look what you did to my face!"

Detective Kim stepped in between them, creating a human wall. Officer Hartman held back the cursing and kicking woman. Amanda was too stunned to move as she stared at Sally. Her head was still smoking; she was missing a diagonal stripe of hair from behind one ear, almost to her forehead, and one eyebrow was shaved completely off.

Another officer turned up to restrain the angry woman, and the officer clamped cuffs on Sally's wrists. With the help of the EMT, they got her onto a gurney and into the ambulance.

Only when Sally's ambulance took off was Amanda able to breathe a sigh of relief.

Dr. Klimmer marched up to them, shaking with rage. "This has been a complete waste of my time! Grok took off. He wouldn't let me near him. He was moving fine and didn't appear to have any wounds other than some scrapes. I'm going home." The man turned around and left, driving away in his long white hearse.

"Okay." With his unflappable manner, Detective Kim asked, "What happened tonight?"

Amanda slumped back on the steps of her ambulance and told the detective about waking up to a sound and confronting the arsonist. "Sally might think I know more than I do. She said that Alexandra had interfered with her plan. The first tart was delivered to me, but Sally thought I was Alexandra and she thought Alexandra and Vik were having an affair. She said she 'taught him a lesson.' I think she killed him."

"Sally has a rock-solid alibi. She was three hundred miles away at the time of the poisoning. She arrived in LA on the 17th and stayed through the 20th with family. On the 21st, she drove back early and immediately filed a report that Vik was missing. Made a lot of noise about it. We believe the poison tart was ingested on the 18th. The family saw her that morning. We have receipts for a shopping trip in the afternoon, and then she was seen by family again in the evening.

Amanda stiffened. That didn't sound right. "Don't you mean for the 16th?"

"No. Why do you think it was the 16th?" The detective studied Amanda's face.

"I saw a parking tag for an LA mall in the window of her SUV that said the 16th. I normally wouldn't remember the date, but that's Alexandra and my birthday; I am 100 percent sure the parking tag said she was at the mall on the 16th. Maybe she went on both dates?"

The detective was flipping through pages in his notebook. "That is interesting. According to her, she wasn't in LA then."

"I think she tried to set up Colleen for the murder. I know I saw rainbow-colored Wellington boots in the back of Sally's car the day after Vik died."

The detective frowned. "The boots match the prints we found around your house. And we can tell from the prints that it was a much smaller foot inside the boots. But we confiscated those boots from Colleen's house, we assumed she had left the prints."

"And did Colleen know anything about them?" Amanda asked.

"She claims to have never seen them before." The detective made a note in his pad.

"What if Alexandra's security system recorded something? The camera in the backyard clearly shows the back of Sally and Vik's house. Maybe Sally slipped back into the house to kill Viktor. And soon after that, I logged into the network and started getting images of the house. Sally knew about that—they were streaming on my phone one day when I was visiting her. That must have been how she learned about the cameras. She kept saying she wanted my phone." Amanda pulled the device out of her pocket. "Do you think they were stored here?"

Detective Kim took Amanda's phone. "I can have the tech guys look at it. All the cameras we've found had their memory drives removed, and the network device from the attic has been damaged. It functions but can't store anything."

"So, with Alexandra gone, if my phone did store the images, I may have the only proof that Sally erased the other security footage." Things were starting to make sense to Amanda. Suddenly, she grabbed the detective's arm, panic spreading through her. "Alexandra's phone would have the images too. Do you think she did anything to hurt Alexandra?"

Detective Kim pat her arm. "She wouldn't have tried to kill Alexandra, you, with the tart if she already knew something had happened to her."

"That's right, thank goodness she tried to kill me!" Amanda sagged back.

The detective looked worried. "Are you going to be okay if I leave you? I need to get tech started on your phone and get to the hospital and question Sally."

"I'll stay with her. You go." Chief Rodriguez walked

up to the back of the ambulance. Frowning, she surveyed the scene.

Amanda swallowed. She had come to the end of her 48 hours. She hadn't found her sister and hadn't filled her van's tank with gas so she could move it. She was not looking forward to talking to the chief.

FORTY

The Rest of the Story

"I'll stay." Frank jogged over from where he had been talking to a firefighter. He had pulled on a navy-blue golf shirt that his husband had brought out for him. It didn't match his rainbow pajama pants or the crocs he was wearing.

"I can stay with her too." They all turned to see Colleen tentatively approach the group. "I've got a lot of explaining to do."

Detective Kim looked conflicted as if he couldn't decide if Colleen's story would be more valuable to record first or Sally's.

"You go. I'll bring Colleen to the station later." Chief Rodriguez volunteered.

"Thanks, chief." The detective ran for his car.

Colleen glanced down at her hands and mumbled. "I owe you an apology, Amanda." She sighed, then peeked up at Amanda, her voice sheepish. "I had nothing to do with Vik's death, but I had been meeting him at Alexandra's when she was gone. I suspect she knew something was going on in the house. And I was right; she put cameras in the rooms. She is never going to forgive me."

"What happened that night?" The chief asked, prodding her back to the topic.

"I was stupid to get involved with Vik again. We dated in high school, and Sally stole him away. I should have considered it a lucky escape. But Mick and I were having trouble, and it seemed so exciting to sneak around. The excitement wore off fast. I told Vik we were done. But he said he would tell my husband we had been having an affair if I didn't keep meeting him."

"Seems like a motive for murder." Frank piped into the conversation. The chief glared him down, and the older man fell silent.

"And what happened that night?" The chief repeated.

"I was in the middle of dying my hair when he called. I didn't want to meet him. But Vik had seen my husband leave, so he knew I was alone. He had been sick for days, and his wife was coming back. He wanted just one more—well, you know. I was so mad. So, to show him it was over, I nipped over while the dye was sitting in my hair. He hates, hated, the smell. I ended up leaving it in way too long." The woman pointed up to the vibrant green hue of her hair.

"And what happened then?" The chief repeated.

Amanda wondered if the chief's patience was why she was on the force.

Colleen picked up her story. "When I got there and found him dead, I panicked. Then Amanda came in, and I completely freaked out. I thought I'd been caught. But then, she left. I shut the front door, dragged Vik into the office chair, strapped him in, and wheeled him out the back door. I didn't want to take him back to my place, so I put him in your van and hid in my yard."

"That's why he had your hair dye on his hand." Amanda jumped up, grabbed her throbbing head, and sat again.

"Probably." Colleen's head bobbed lower.

Frank looked puzzled. "I still don't understand why you took the body out of the van?"

"I wasn't thinking clearly. After I put him there, I realized if Amanda had just arrived, the body would be even more suspicious in her van. So, after she left to call the police again, I moved him to the bed of my husband's truck. He hadn't been able to start it and had taken my car to work that evening."

"How did you get him in there?" Frank looked Colleen up and down.

"I do a lot of yoga! And I rolled him over in the chair and then just kept rolling him to get him in. I couldn't get the tailgate closed, but Mick keeps a tarp in the back, so I covered Vik and the chair up." As they all stared at her, Colleen added with a sniff. "Well, I didn't know Mick had taken an extra morning shift, and before I could figure out where to move Vik's body, Mick had jump-started the truck and left for work. I don't know what happened after that." Colleen planted her forehead in her hand, and after a second, she peeked out at the chief. "How much trouble am I in?"

"A lot, but if you help us, it'll look better for you." Chief Rodriguez gave Colleen a warning.

"Surely this is enough to clear Alexandra of any wrongdoing," Amanda asked the chief.

The chief pursed her lips, then shook her head, "I never thought Alexandra had anything to do with this—except put up the cameras. And that tells me she was planning on being gone and keeping an eye on the house."

Amanda didn't follow what the chief meant. "Wait, you think she has been watching the house and me?"

"I'm pretty sure she would have called if she knew you were here." The chief said.

"So, can we finally start looking for her?" Amanda begged.

"Already working on it." The chief turned at a commotion.

Amanda followed the chief's gaze in time to see Ben arrive. His eyes wide, he reached out a hand to Amanda. "I heard you were attacked by the killer and set on fire!"

"The van was set on fire, not me. I'm fine. Mostly." She assured him, squeezing his hand back, and then, self-conscious of everyone watching, released it.

A motorcycle zoomed down the street towards them and parked in Frank's driveway. Dot hopped off the bike and removed her helmet before heading to their group.

"Colleen, come to the station with me now. Amanda, you can stay with Ben and come by in the morning to make your statement." The chief ended the discussion and led Colleen away.

"It looks like I missed quite a lot," Dot said, studying

the scene. "Why does your van look like a burnt pink marshmallow? And what happened to its ears?"

Amanda wanted to cry.

The van was a mess. Even if it were operational, nobody would want to get their dog groomed in a vehicle that looked like it had been in a bonfire.

"There, there, dear. Don't worry about it now. You come over to my house and spend the night. You can tell me all about it in the morning." Dot took charge, directing Ben to bring Amanda to her house.

Ben nodded in agreement.

Dot patted Amanda's hand, telling her she would see her soon, then stalked back to her bike.

Nobody asked Amanda what she thought, but she was rather relieved not to have to make any decisions.

Ben guided her to his car and opened the front passenger door. Grok suddenly appeared and immediately jumped into the front seat. He glared at Ben until he shut the front door and opened the back door for Amanda. She half sat, and half collapsed into the seat. Glad to have the night over.

Back in Business

The next morning, Amanda and Ben stood in Alexandra's front yard and surveyed the damage. Last night, the fire department had drenched the van, putting out the fire. They and the police department had trampled the little patch of flowers and traipsed mud across the porch and down the sidewalk. The jewel in the middle of the mud pie was the Pink Pup. Most of its ears were gone, and the van looked more like a terrier now, with one ear sticking up from the top and the other folded over.

The top and upper sides of the vehicle had fared okay. You could still see the dog's face and the name of the grooming service, but the bottom was scorched, and the graphic wrap melted and warped. Dot was right. It did look like a burnt pink marshmallow.

Amanda leaned closer. "Hey, look at that. The fire burnt off my ex's phone number."

"Well, there's a bright side." Ben followed her as she walked around the van. "You know what, I'm going to see if there's a rake, and I can get rid of the rest of these leaves."

Ben trotted off to check in the shed.

Amanda slid open the door of the van. Relieved to find out everything inside was intact. She turned on the water system and checked out the pump and generator.

Everything still worked!

She should still be able to do her business if anyone was interested in her services after this.

Amanda stepped out of the van again to find Detective Kim talking with Ben.

"Do you have a minute?" The detective asked in a tone that implied it wasn't a question.

"Yes. I am unlikely to be busy for a while. What happened with Sally last night?"

"She is in custody. I investigated the parking ticket date. You were right. She had been to the mall on the 16th and had altered her receipts to look like they were from the 18th. She didn't have an alibi."

"But can you drive to LA and back in one day?" Amanda asked.

"You can. We think she found out Viktor had drained their joint bank account and was planning on leaving her, so she timed it to arrive and hide in the house while he was out foraging. He got home and followed his routine of baking wild mushroom tarts and going out for celebration drinks with his friends." Detective Kim looked down at his notes.

"This was the group that got food poisoning?" Ben asked.

"Yes. That's why it was hard to track the members down; they've been sick. While he was out drinking, she must've switched the tarts with ones she premade. Their garage freezer had traces of death cap in it. After the switch, she drove back to LA, and when her family got home late from the event, she was already in bed. They thought she was there the whole time." The detective flipped closed his notebook.

There was one thing Amanda still couldn't figure out. "But if he was sick, why would he want to meet Colleen at Alexandra's house?"

Ben leaned the rake against the side of the house. "It would have taken 6-12 hours for symptoms to kick in, and by then, it would have been too late. He might have thought his symptoms were food poisoning, like everyone else on the trip. A bout of terminal lucidity is not uncommon with this type of poisoning. He probably called Colleen when he was feeling better and arranged to meet her at the house, then rapidly declined after he got there."

"Did Sally say why she tried to kill me?"

"First, it was misidentification. She didn't know if your sister or Colleen was the one having an affair with her husband. She knew they were meeting here. When she returned to town, she delivered an anonymous gift basket with one of the tarts to Alexandra—you. Vik wasn't in the house when she got home, so if caught with the basket she could pretend she didn't know the tarts were poisoned." The detective said.

"So that is why the mess of the tart on the porch disappeared," Amanda remembered being puzzled as to where it had gone.

"When she realized her mistake, she destroyed the evidence and tried to set Colleen up for killing Vik, leaving the boots and the dried mushrooms at her house. Then she was after you because of this." Detective Kim pulled her phone from his pocket.

"No one knew that Alexandra had put in those cameras and that the one in the backyard showed the back of Sally's house. Your phone had images of her hunting for the cameras and breaking into the house. There was also a camera that none of us found that clearly showed her attacking you and trying to set the van and house on fire—hoping to destroy any other evidence."

Amanda shivered. If it weren't for Grok, she'd be dead twice.

"It's incredibly dangerous to cook with death caps. She's lucky she didn't poison herself." Ben added.

"Maybe that's why she threw out all the baking pans afterward." Amanda guessed.

"Well, she has a lawyer and has stopped talking, but it's too late. We now have the evidence. She is being booked for premeditated murder and charges for her attack on you. Just wanted to let you know you are safe now."

Amanda felt a sense of relief at Detective Kim's statement. She followed him to his car to sign for and receive her phone and the casebook.

"I should let you know that the tech team blocked the phone number that was constantly calling and texting you.

I can show you how to unblock the number." The detective reached for the phone.

Amanda held the phone behind her back. "Not necessary. I should have blocked that number a long time ago."

The detective shrugged and left

She returned to where Ben was waiting for her.

"What are you going to do now?" Ben asked, his eyes guarded.

"I guess I'll find a job until Alexandra returns and either meets me or kicks me out of town. I don't think she is on a work trip. I want to know what happened to her. Even if the chief can't find her, I will keep looking." Amanda wasn't sure how long that would be.

"Hello? Are you the groomer?" A woman stood on the sidewalk looking over the white picket fence, an apricot Royal Poodle on a leash at her side.

"I am a groomer. Can I help you?" Amanda stepped forward eagerly.

Ben tapped her on the shoulder and whispered in her ear. "Meet you for dinner later?"

Amanda nodded and then headed to the woman at the fence.

"Buddy looks amazing. Katrina told us all about you. I wanted to get here before you got all booked up for the day. Please tell me you have time to fit my Noodles in?"

Amanda opened the gate and ushered the woman in, eager to get started.

FORTY-TWO

Special

Amanda was busy all day as one client after another turned up. Around lunchtime, a man in a tow truck pulled up with a German Shepherd in the passenger seat. The man explained the German shepherd was his sidekick, but he was so busy with work that he hadn't had time to bathe him, and the dog had gotten so stinky the Shepard would have to stay home soon. The man begged her to find room for a same-day appointment. Amanda skipped lunch and squeezed in a bath for the shepherd.

While the tow truck driver waited, he added gas to her tank. She could make it up to the filling station now. And after today, she'd have enough money for it.

Finally, in the late afternoon, the foot traffic died down. Ben called and told her where to meet him and Dot for dinner. Amanda realized she had enough time for a walk on the beach. She closed shop before anyone else could drop by and, with Grok beside her, walked the 20 minutes to the shore.

Waves crash against rocks, spraying the path ahead of them. The bright blue sky reached the horizon, meeting the gray-blue ocean. Sailboats and fishing boats dotted the water, along with flocks of birds diving for fish.

Amanda and Grok wove in and out of other walkers as they followed the gravel path alongside the rocky shore. They got a few stares, and a couple of kids stopped to take photos.

Amanda finally worked up the nerve to talk to the cat.

"Okay, I know you can understand me. Right?" Amanda felt very silly for asking. Even though she always talked to her dog clients, she didn't expect them to talk back.

Grok stopped and looked up at her. Amanda swore there was a grin on the cat's face.

Impulsively, Amanda said, "Nod once for yes and twice for no?"

"No," Grok said. Amanda heard the word clearly in her head.

"No, you can't talk to me, or you can't understand me?" Amanda realized how ridiculous those questions were even as she asked them.

Grok snorted and started walking again.

Amanda resumed talking. "I'm not crazy. You can talk. But I hear you in my head. Can you read my thoughts? Can you talk to everyone or just me? Could you talk to my sister too? Do you understand anyone else? Can you talk in full sentences or just one word? Have you been able to do this all your life?" Amanda had so many questions.

Grok shook his head. "I think I preferred the quiet.

Your human mind is so fractured I'm impressed you can dress yourself each morning." He strutted further down the path. They passed by other people who didn't seem to even hear the cat. "You are just talking. Everyone can hear you. What is remarkable is that you can hear me. Alexandra could too. She was the only one until I met you. I suspect that your monozygotic brains are both receptive to me psychically."

"Your whole life, you have never talked to anyone else?" Amanda stopped walking and stared down at the cat.

"That may not be as long as you would think. I have no memory of my life before one year ago, when Alexandra found me." The cat stopped. He groaned and looked down in pain.

Amanda dropped to her knees next to the cat. "Are you okay?"

Grok shuddered, then looked up at Amanda. "I am unable to remember where she found me. I know she was trying to investigate where I came from, but whenever I talk or think about it, I get a blinding pain in my head, and sometimes I get dizzy or pass out."

Amanda clearly heard the words in her head and understood that somehow, she and Alexandra could psychically understand the cat, but no one else could.

"Can you tell me how that's possible?" Amanda waited for the cat to respond.

Grok winced. "No. I don't know. I know it's not common here. Where I come from, it's normal to talk this way." Grok gasped and sunk to his belly.

"Okay, let's not talk about that. You think about something happy, like your favorite food, and I'll try and summarize. See if you agree, disagree, or pass on answering." Amanda rubbed a hand over the cat's paw.

"You are not from 'here,' and you don't know where you are from or have any memory older than one year ago," Amanda stated.

"Yes." Grok agreed.

Nothing happened, so Amanda continued. "You understand everyone around you but can only talk to Alexandra and me psychically, not anyone else on this... planet?"

Grok nodded. When he didn't show any pain, he added, "Yes, my translator works on all the human species here. I have no idea what the animals are saying to each other."

Amanda tried to hide that she was freaking out as she soothed the cat's paw. Did he not realize he had just admitted to being from another planet? She decided to push a bit more. "Alexandra is somewhere out there investigating your arrival, but you can't say or think where she is. Can you tell me if she is safe?"

"I don't know. But I'll do everything I can to help you find her." Grok shook his head but was able to stand. "I think you may have found a workaround for the amnesia."

"Well, we aren't learning anything new, but you don't have to hurt yourself telling me things this way. Are you sure there is no one else like you here on Earth?"

Grok started to shake his head, then stopped, "Pass."

"Okay, okay, let's not dig too deep into that right now.

Here's a question for you. Why are you so afraid of the vet?" Amanda laughed at the expression on the cat's face.

Grok gave her a look that said he found her a big, boring, stupid human and strutted off.

Amanda was fine to walk behind him the rest of the way home. She had more to think about than a giant psychic amnesic alien cat.

It had been a very confusing time for her since she had left Ohio. She'd willingly left her ex-husband and her home when she found out what he was doing. Amanda thought of Sally. She had a lot in common with the woman, but they had each made different choices. Amanda had come to California hoping to rekindle a relationship with her sister and make a new start.

Amanda smiled. It was incredible to see what her sister had achieved in Ocean Wood. Everything they had dreamed about as young women. Her sister was so brave she hoped she could be half the woman that Alexandra was.

Amanda realized this was the first time in a long time that she was excited thinking about what came next in her life. She had prospects for work and almost a full tank of gas.

Amanda looked at her phone and turned away from the shore. It was time to head into town for dinner with Ben and Dot. But she would be back to the ocean every chance she got.

"You coming with me?" She asked Grok.

The cat followed her into town.

FORTY-THREE

Friends

Amanda arrived at the Lighthouse pub as Ben was parking. They walked in together. Dot and Albert already had a table by the window.

The couple greeted them, and Ben took drink orders for the table. He made them promise to wait to talk about anything important until he returned.

Albert asked about Amanda's clients, and she told him how Katrina had spread the word and she was now booked up for the week.

"Hey, Dot." Amanda leaned in. "What did you do to Sally and Viktor for making you move your accessibility ramp?"

Albert chuckled.

Dot got a sly look as she replied, "The location of the new ramp runs right by their bedroom window. I've got a friend who raises chickens. One turned out to be a rooster. I recorded it crowing, and we played it randomly throughout the night outside their window. Doesn't bother us. We can't hear it over Albert's CPAP machine."

Amanda shook her head and smiled as Dot burst out giggling.

When Ben returned, Dot slammed down her fist, shaking the table. "Okay, enough jibber jabber. Spill it. What are you going to do now? Are you staying here in town?" The woman demanded of Amanda, then took a gulp of the beer Ben had brought for her as if she was worried the beer would disappear with Amanda.

"Yeah, I want to know, too," Ben added, sipping his wine.

"I want to see my sister. No one seems concerned she is missing, well, the chief is started to look into it. I found her casebook. She was working on four different cases. I think one of them might be related to her being missing." Amanda left out the part that there might be a fifth case, a secret case, about Grok, her sister was investigating.

Grok took that moment to make his presence known. Jumping up on the table, he gave a loud meow. Everyone saved their drinks.

"Sounds like Grok thinks that's a good idea, too." Albert petted the cat, and it preened.

"Do you think my sister would mind me staying in her house until she returns?" Amanda still felt uncertain of her welcome there.

"I wouldn't worry about that." The voice came from the restaurant's door. Chief Rodriguez walked in with a man at her side.

Albert greeted them. "Hi Gina, nice to see you and Mario out. You must've gotten a babysitter?"

Amanda didn't know why she was surprised, but she had never pictured the chief as anything other than a police officer.

"Yep, date night." Chief Rodriguez had the first smile on her face Amanda had ever seen. It disappeared as she turned to Amanda. "You should stay at your sister's house. You have the same knack for trouble as she does, and I will be keeping an eye on you."

The chief and her husband walked away, and Amanda figured it was as close to a "welcome" as she would get from the officer.

"Well, this weekend, we are finally going to clean Alexandra's house so you can stay there." Ben waited for her nod, and then he continued. "And I have some exciting news." Ben paused for effect, then revealed, "I just bought a boat!"

Ben looked so excited. Amanda didn't know what to say. She glanced at Albert and Dot, who were sharing a knowing grimace. Dot said, "Good luck with that."

Oblivious to the side glances from the couple, Ben continued to tell them about his boat. "It was a lucky find. The guy was going to the Naval Postgraduate School and got orders to ship out. He seemed quite eager to get rid of it at a great price. It's a perfect situation. With the boat, I won't have to sell my house in San Francisco. I have good renters, and they are hard to find. And I can move out of the motel into the boat. Qbert will love it."

Their food arrived, and Grok jumped down into a spare chair.

The waiter put plates in front of each of them. They all froze when he placed a large tart in the center of the table.

"Who is that from?" Amanda asked, terrified of the answer.

"The chief sent it to the table and said I was to let you know—it's a lemon tart. Made in-house."

The server left, and they all sighed with relief, but no one ate the tart.

THE END...

But what about that pink sweater? Read a bonus chapter at https://www.serengoode.com/cozybooks-nlt

Keep reading for an excerpt from *Monterey Bay Murder*, Book 2 of the Amanda Warren Cozy Animal Mystery Series, ***available now!***

When Amanda and Grok arrived at the library, Ms. Meyers gave them a stern look as she held the door open. She quickly led them past the staff desk, the book stacks, reading room and through another set of doors to a glassed-in meeting room. The children's brightly lit reading area was in the corner of this space, and it looked like an event was happening. Dozens of small children clustered around a colorful carpet with a giant bean bag.

Ms. Meyers pointed in the direction of the event. Her lips twitched, and the stern look dissolved into a big smile. "He's been very popular with our young patrons, but perhaps it's time he went home."

A small girl, four or five years old, spotted them as they approached the group. One pigtail had freed itself, and she was wearing a miniature neon fireman's jacket with a rainbow tutu, butterfly wings, and a manic expression. She pulled her thumb out of her mouth with a pop and pointed a wet finger at Grok. "Look! Big kitty!"

Grok froze. He started to back away as if a bear had spotted him. But it was too late. A group of toddlers attacked. They tugged at his fur, swung his tail like a jump rope, and several declared he was big enough to ride like a pony.

As the group magnetized to Grok, Amanda saw what had been holding their attention. Qbert was lying on the bean bag in the center of the reading area. At least six children were using the dog as a pillow, and dozens of colorful elastic bands and barrettes styled his fur.

When Amanda approached him, Qbert had a blissed-out look from the attention. She snapped the lead on his collar and tugged on the leash. Several children cried out in dismay, and one burst into tears.

"Sorry, but Qbert has to go home now." Amanda backed towards the door, unsure if turning her back on the emotional mini humans was safe. She groaned when she realized she was starting to sound like the grumpy cat. That reminded her, and she called out, "Come on, Grok."

The large cat exploded from the surrounding group, almost levitating in his haste to escape.

Ms. Meyers walked them out. "Thank you for coming, but maybe it would be best if you don't return, this visit has been too stimulating for the younger patrons."

With a nod, she ushered Amanda and the animals out of the library. The door slid shut behind them.

Monterey Bay Murder, Book 2 of the Amanda Warren Cozy Animal Mystery Series, is a fur-raising whodunit as dog groomer Amanda Warren and Grok, her talking cat, dive nose-first into another whisker-twitching mystery! Available now.

Other books by Seren Goode
The Elements Series (Young Adult)
The Keystone
The Activator
The Amanda Warren Cozy Animal Mystery Series (Mystery)
Monterey Bay Mystery
Monterey Bay Murder

Acknowledgments

It takes a lot of support to be an author and I want to thank all my family and friends that have helped me along the way. I especially want to thank Randy for always having my back. Amy C. for the coaching and cohosting. My Tropetastic friends. Hannah J. for editing and the tough talks. And my personal cheerleader who got me into this whole cozy business and is the most fabulous beta reader and friend, Lori H. Thank you!

Thank you!

Your comments and feedback are so important to me and they help other readers select a book they will enjoy. **If you liked this book, please spread the word! Leave a review** on the platform where you bought it or on **Goodreads** or **Bookbub**. And thank you for telling your friends and posting on social!

We would love to have you join our community of cozy mystery readers. Sign-up to engage, share ideas, receive news, hear about future books, get free stories and lots of fun stuff through (mostly) monthly emails...and no spam. https://www.serengoode.com/cozybooks-nlt.

And if you love talking about the books you read, then consider joining the COZY MYSTERY BOOKS REVIEW (ARC) TEAM. You can sign-up at https://www.serengoode.com/contact

I sincerely appreciate your support and would love to hear from you at SerenGoodWrites on:

Contact https://www.serengoode.com/contact
Goodreads http://bit.ly/Goodreads_SerenGoode
Bookbub http://bit.ly/BookBub_SerenGoode
Instagram instagram.com/serengoodewrites
TikTok tiktok.com/@serengoodewrites
Facebook facebook.com/SerenGoode
Pinterest pinterest.com/SerenGoodeWrites

Seren Goode was born in the Midwest with itchy feet and a dream of far-off places. She loves travel and walking on the beach (hot or cold). And no matter where she is in the world her favorite thing is to curl up with a good cozy mystery and a hot cup of tea.

A Jane-of-all-trades, Seren has studied communications, English, design, marketing, metalsmith, pottery, juggling, and more, and eventually ended up abroad earning a graduate degree in archeology. She started writing fiction while in middle school and thoroughly blames her family for encouraging this habit. A big fan of making her characters do their own work, Seren loves to sit back and watch them unravel a mystery or dig for the truth. When she isn't on the road, she is at home on the Central Coast of California plotting her next book, and her next trip, with her songwriter husband and puppies Clairey and Izzy.

You can follow her at serengoode.com or on:
facebook.com/SerenGoode
instagram.com/serengoodewrites
pinterest.com/SerenGoodeWrites
tiktok.com/@serengoodewrites

Monterey Bay Mystery

Written and published by Seren Goode

Cover by Mariah Sinclair & Associates

Formatting by Goode Star

Ebook ISBN: 978-1-7365387-6-0

Print ISBN: 978-1-7365387-7-7

SerenGoode.com

9 781736 538777